The Last of the OGs 2
Penitentiary Gangstas

Tranay Adams

Lock Down Publications and Ca$h Presents
The Last of the OGs 2
A Novel by *Tranay Adams*

The Last of the OGs 2

Lock Down Publications
P.O. Box 944
Stockbridge, Ga 30281
www.lockdownpublications.com

Copyright 2021 Tranay Adams
The Last of the OGs 2

Lock Down Publications
Like our page on Facebook: Lock Down Publications @
www.facebook.com/lockdownpublications.ldp
Cover design and layout by: **Dynasty Cover Me**
Book interior design by: **Shawn Walker**
Edited by: **Tamira Butler**

Stay Connected with Us!

Text **LOCKDOWN** to 22828 to stay up-to-date with new
releases, sneak peaks, contests and more…
Thank you!

Submission Guideline.

Submit the first three chapters of your completed manuscript to ldpsubmissions@gmail.com, subject line: Your book's title. The manuscript must be in a .doc file and sent as an attachment. Document should be in Times New Roman, double spaced and in size 12 font. Also, provide your synopsis and full contact information. If sending multiple submissions, they must each be in a separate email.

Have a story but no way to send it electronically? You can still submit to LDP/Ca$h Presents. Send in the first three chapters, written or typed, of your completed manuscript to:

LDP: Submissions Dept
P.O. Box 944
Stockbridge, Ga 30281

DO NOT send original manuscript. Must be a duplicate.

Provide your synopsis and a cover letter containing your full contact information.

Thanks for considering LDP and Ca$h Presents.

Tranay Adams

Chapter One
Las Vegas/Penthouse suite

Hitt-Man held her ass cheeks apart as he pounded away at her warm, gooey center. Her twat occasionally farted with each of his thrusts, and a ripple traveled up her chunky bottom. The smell of sex and the sound of clapping filled the air every time his hot, sweaty body collided with hers.

"Ahhh, fuck, faster, faster!" the Somalian dimepiece called out in between eating his wife's pussy. Her head and her perfectly shaped, dark-brown areola breasts bounced up and down with each plunge of Hitt-Man's thick endowment. The dopeman's dick glistened from the flow of her womb's natural secretions.

"Ssssssss," Niqua hissed like a venomous serpent while the dimepiece was sucking on the small flap of meat nestled between her sex lips. The spectacular sensation was driving her wild. She could literally feel the muscles of her kitty contract and spill its juices. "Mmmmmm! Yes, yessss, fuck!" she egged on the bitch that was sucking on her clit and fingering her. She clenched and unclenched her jaws, which caused veins to bulge on her forehead. "Ah, ah, ah, ah!" She humped into her mouth and then bit down on her bottom lip.

Niqua was a chocolate goddess that held an uncanny resemblance to Keisha in the movie *Belly*, except her tits and ass were enhanced, thanks to the best plastic surgeon in Beverly Hills. Shorty was inked from her neck, to her arms, to her thighs. Her navel and clit were pierced with genuine diamonds. All of these attributes accompanied by her short Cleopatra hairstyle and Egyptian style of makeup made her look like the African American female rappers of today.

Niqua licked her full lips and manipulated one of her nipples since her other hand was holding a bottle of Cristal. She looked down at shorty that was giving her dome and then back up at Hitt-Man. Watching her husband dick down the bitch eating her pussy turned her the fuck on. She couldn't get enough of the shit! He puckered his lips up at her and she puckered hers back up at him.

She guzzled some of the champagne, spilling it down her chin. She wiped it away and looked down at the dimepiece who was feasting on her treasure. She poured some of the tasty liquid on her flat stomach. It formed a small river as it flowed down her torso and washed over her vagina. The Somalian dimepiece sucked up some of the bubbly, but Hitt-Man was stroking her so good she looked back at him.

"Just like that! Oh, yes, just like that!" the Somalian dimepiece hollered as Hitt-Man sped up his back shots. His locs bounced as he moved his hips back and forth. The wet clapping sound grew louder and louder, and the smell of sex became heavier inside the suite.

The two million dollars in icy gold jewelry bounced up and down on Hit-Man's shiny, tattooed chest. Sweat leaped from his muscular form and splashed upon her back and ass. The dopeman had a mad dog expression on his face as he plowed into the dimepiece. He smacked her on her booty again, then he sucked on his thumb, making sure it was nice and dripping with his spit. Without warning, he shoved it up the dimepiece's asshole and drew a sensual whine from her.

"You like that shit, huh?" Hitt-Man asked as he watched himself go in and out of the Somalian dimepiece's twat. She was cumming so much that white shit was coating more and more of his dick.

"Oh, yes, yes! I like it, I fucking love it!" the Somalian dimepiece called out with a jovial look on her face. Hitt-Man continued to give her that gangsta dick raw and uncut like he knew her old rat ass liked it. He looked up at Niqua with his locs hanging over his face. All she could see past his locs were his tormented eyes. They made him look like a straight-up beast. She held his intense gaze while he continued to beat that dime bitch's back up.

Hitt-Man knew how much his wife got off to him smashing bitchez in front of her. That shit made her horny enough to bust on the spot! Niqua's hardened nipples and erect clit made this apparent.

"Ah, ah, ah, ah, fuck, y—yes!" The Somalian dimepiece's eyes rolled and her mouth hung open. Hitt-Man saw she wasn't eating his wife's pussy, and that made him mad. He loved busting down a new bitch, but he enjoyed it more knowing his wife was being satisfied too.

"Bitch, shut the fuck up and eat my queen's pussy!" Hitt-Man demanded and mashed her face into his wife's bald twat. He grinned wickedly seeing Niqua squirm and lick her lips, enjoying getting her clit manipulated. She wrapped her legs around the dimepiece's neck. The bitch was sucking on her jewel, fingering her savagely while rubbing on her own shit.

Ain't no fun if wifey can't have none, Hitt-Man thought, looking at the pleasured expression written across his queen's face.

"That's right, ho, eat my shit—eat this pussy!" Niqua whined sensually, rotating and tweaking her nipple. She passed the bottle of Cristal to her husband and focused on her nipples. Her pretty, French-tip-manicured toes curled and her eyes rolled back. Niqua, using her diamond-pierced tongue, licked her top row of teeth erotically. "Uh, uh, uh, uh, uh, uh!" She grabbed a handful of the Somalian dimepiece's hair and threw her head back. She could feel her orgasm building up and up. It felt like she had to piss really, really bad, but that definitely wasn't the case. Niqua stared up at their reflections courtesy of the mirrored ceiling. She observed her husband pour champagne on the bitch they were flipping back and then drink from it thirstily.

Hitt-Man switched hands with the Cristal bottle and occasionally smacked the Somalian dimepiece on her ass as he stroked her from the back. More sweat oozed out of his pores, sliding down his chest, rock-hard abs, and hairy, muscular buttocks.

"Yeah, bitch, eat the royal pussy while the king fucks you from the back!" Hitt-Man commanded and gave her butt another hard smack. Her ass cheek jiggled and a red hand impression appeared. Holding the bottle in his hand, he fucked her from the back faster and made her booty jump. The faster he attacked her from that angle, the wetter she got and the harder she rubbed her clit.

"Uh, uh, uh, uh!" the Somalian dimepiece hollered out with a scrunched face.

"Oooooh, oh! Oh! Oh, shiiit!" Niqua's faced balled up in bliss, and she mashed that bitch's face back into her pussy.

"Eat me, bitch! Eat me!" Niqua urged her. She could feel her orgasm coming ahead, and her legs were shaking. Her ghetto, sexy ass looked like a volcano on the verge of erupting. "I'm 'bouta cum, I'm 'bouta cum!"

"Mmmmmm—mmmmm!" the Somalian dimepiece said with a mouthful of Niqua's phat pussy. Shorty was trying to say 'I'm 'bouta cum' like Niqua. The queen was holding her in place now. She couldn't move an inch, and she wasn't going to until little mama popped off.

"Shit, this pussy tight! On Blood gang, I'm 'bouta bust!" Hitt-Man claimed, balling his face. He could feel his nuts swelling and semen building in his shit. The penthouse suite filled with moans and groans of all the participants in the threesome. The closer they all got to getting off, the louder the moans and groans became until they exploded.

"Aaaahh, fuuuuuuck!" Niqua hollered out and sprayed the dimepiece's face. She then fell flat out on the bed. Her eyes were narrowed and her mouth was open. Her entire body shook like she was a death-row inmate in an electric chair.

"Shhiiiiiiit!" the Somalian dimepiece hollered with bulging eyes and a wide-open mouth. Her juices flooded her thighs as she reached her orgasm. She started shaking just like Niqua and fell flat on her stomach. That didn't stop Hitt-Man from climbing on top of her and placing his fists on either side of her. He pumped her six fast, hard times and bust deep inside of her. Warm, clear globs of his gooey semen splashed against her pink walls. Exhausted, he fell on the side of her on the bed. He lay there hot and sweaty with a thudding heart and semi-hard dick.

"Goddamn. That shit hit the spot!" Hitt-Man emphasized 'spot' and smacked the dimepiece on her ass. She jumped from the sting of the smack, whimpered, and started dozing off to sleep.

"What's up, queen? How was it?" He looked toward the head of the bed at Niqua.

"Shit was decent," Niqua replied, exhausted, with a thudding heart. She sat up, looked at homegirl while she was snoring, and kicked that bitch out of the bed. She hollered in freefall before she collided with the carpeted floor. "It's time for you to go, love."

Niqua hopped out of bed and slipped on her kimono, tying it around her waist. She left the bedroom and came back with a glass of water and a Plan-B pill. When she returned, Hitt-Man was sitting on the edge of the bed while old girl was climbing back up on her bare feet.

"Here you go." Niqua passed her the glass and the pill. She folded her arms across her chest and tapped her foot impatiently. She eyeballed homegirl as she tossed back the pill and washed it down. The girl sat the empty glass down on the nightstand and turned to Niqua, asking for her money for the sex. "Hol' up."

Niqua walked around the bed and tilted the chick's head back. Using her finger, she felt around inside of her mouth and then looked down inside of it. She didn't see the pill.

"Alright. You can get dressed," Niqua told her as she walked away. She put in the combination to the black safe that came with their room, and it opened automatically. Inside, there were stacks and stacks of blue faces with rubber bands around them. She snatched out one and closed the safe. She then took the rubber band from around the dead presidents and counted off two gees. She folded it and held it out to homegirl as she approached her, slipping on her pump. She took it and placed it inside of her bra.

"I'll show you out," Niqua told her as she guided her toward the door.

"Wait, here's my card." The dimepiece gave her a black business card in case she wanted her services again. Niqua glanced at it and continued to guide her toward the door. Once she saw the girl out, she shut and locked the door behind her.

Niqua tore up the black card as she journeyed towards the bedroom. She threw the torn up pieces of card into the trashcan. She and Hitt-Man never flipped the same bitchez twice. That was never any fun. As she crossed the threshold of the bedroom, she could hear the shower running. She shook her head when she noticed her husband's pile of necklaces, watches, bracelets, and rings on the nightstand. For some strange reason, he enjoyed fucking while rocking all of his jewels. He called it Rich Sex, which made no fucking sense to her.

I done told this ol' big head husband of mine to keep his money and jewels inside the safe. The maids at these hotels have the keys to get into the guests' rooms, and these bitchez be stealing shit! Let's not forget those fools that were scoping us out down at the craps table earlier tonight. Dwayne thinks they were eyeballing me, but something tells me they were peeping all the chips he'd racked up and all the ice he was rocking. You can't tell his big ass shit, though. Ughh! Men! Niqua thought as she deposited her man's jewelry inside the safe along with the stacks of dead presidents. She shut the door to the safe and made her way toward the bathroom. As soon as she crossed the threshold, she peeled off her robe and hung it on the hook on the back of the door. The bathroom was humid and foggy from the hot water spraying from the shower nozzle.

Niqua shut the bathroom door and made her way toward the glass enclosure that housed the shower. The glass was running with beads of water, and it was foggy. She could still make out Hitt-Man's nakedness as he lathered himself up with soap. Niqua opened the door of the shower and stepped in. She took the loofa from her man and went about the task of washing him up. He shut his eyes and bowed his head. He then placed his hands on the wall and allowed her to cater to him like the street king he was.

Hitt-Man was a multi-millionaire since Caleb was no longer in the picture. He continued to push his poison in the streets until it was all gone. Then, he collected the profit he'd made from it, added the dollars to it he had put up and the loot Caleb had in his secret stash. He went to the same Chinese restaurant to holla at Wang Lei and got the run around. A day later, Wang contacted him. They met up at another location and made a deal for four hundred birds of that raw. After that night, Hitt-Man took off and never looked back. He had more money than he knew what to do with and an army of assassins at his disposal.

"Baby, turn around for me so I can get cho front," Niqua told him. As soon as he did, she started lathering up his rock-hard body.

"Don't forget to clean the royal dick while you're at it," Hitt-Man told her, watching her scrub every inch of his body.

"Yes, king," Niqua replied, washing up his dick and balls. She frowned, noticing the faraway look in his eyes. "What's wrong?"

"You know, it's crazy, they say God works in mysterious ways," Hitt-Man began. "I prayed to 'em to show me a way to get rich. With the death of my best friend, I winded up taking over his business. Now, here I am—a millionaire hood nigga. I got cars, clothes, jewels up the ass, flying in private jets, and fucking the women of other niggaz' dreams," he claimed as the hot liquid rinsed the soap off his form.

"Lemme guess, you'd give it all up to have your best friend back?" Niqua asked before she started sucking on his nut sack and jerking his dick.

Hitt-Man closed his eyes and held his head back. He licked his lips and began moaning upon feeling Niqua's juicy mouth on his piece. He thought about what she'd asked him before she started giving him fellatio. Would he give up all he'd obtained so Caleb could be alive again?

No! Hell no! I love this shit, Hitt-Man thought, grunting as he was getting his dick sucked. He looked down at Niqua, and she was staring at him while she fingered herself. He put his hand on her head and started fucking her mouth aggressively.

"Ack, ack, ack, ack!" Niqua gagged and choked.

"Mmmmm, mmmmm," Hitt-Man moaned as he thrust in and out her mouth. "Shit feels good, real good," he claimed, feeling Niqua massage his nutsack while she played with herself. She was so turned on by his moaning and grunting that her pussy started raining. Her body shook like she was in a massage chair having reached an orgasm. She continued to diddle herself, causing more and more rain to fall.

I gotta make sure I show out for 'em tonight. Maybe that way he won't want to keep inviting other bitchez in our bed, Niqua thought as she kept going with her sexual performance. *At this point, I'm desperate. I'll do anything to keep him. A bitch may be old, but I still gotta couple tricks in my bag.*

"Ack, ack, ack, ack!" Niqua's gagging and choking filled the bathroom. She became teary eyed, snot began to ooze out of her nose, and she was slobbering heavy. In fact, an avalanche of her bubbling saliva slid down her neck and onto her chest.

"Yeah—yeah, that shit feels bomb as fuck witchu massaging my shit," Hitt-Man told her. To him, it was nothing like having a fine ass bitch sucking your dick—that was some boss ass shit! "That's right, bitch, uh, I mean, baby, you're right where you're 'pose to be—at the feet of your king."

Niqua sucked off Hitt-Man for a few minutes longer and then popped him out of her mouth. She stared up at him seductively while stroking his dick up and down with both hands. A frown was fixed on his face as he wondered why she'd stopped sucking his piece. She read his mind and answered him before he could even ask.

"I wanna try something else, your royal highness," Niqua told him, with slimy strings of saliva dangling from her lips and chin. She was stroking her husband with both hands the entire time she was speaking to him.

"Something like what?" Hitt-Man asked with furrowed brows.

"You'll see, king. Now turn around." Niqua smiled kinkily as she motioned for him to turn around. Hitt-Man reluctantly turned around then shrugged like, now what? "Put cho hands against the wall and spread yo' legs like the police finna pat chu down," she ordered him as she got up on her bare feet.

"Niqua, I'm telling you right now, don't chu shove yo' thumb up my ass," Hitt-Man said, with seriousness. "I'm not with none of that faggot ass shit. I'll fuck around and karate chop yo' black ass in the throat."

Niqua laughed as she approached him. "Ain't nobody finna shove nothing up yo' ass, Dewayne, relax. Lemme do what I do."

Hitt-Man took a deep breath and assumed the position Niqua had told him to. He felt awkward being in such a vulnerable position, but he still granted her request anyway. Niqua rubbed up and down his arms as she placed gentle kisses down his back. She continued kissing down his back until she was on her knees facing his ass.

"Bend over," Niqua told him as she rubbed on his buttocks.

"Baby, I just told you I'm not with—"

"I know what you said, babe. And I'm not finna do that," she assured him. "Now bend that ass over." She smacked him on his right cheek. He started to call the whole thing off, but he was curious as to what she wanted to try on him. He took a breath and bent over, leaving her looking at his crinkle, nutsack, and dick hanging between his muscular legs. "There you go. See, now that wasn't that hard, was it?"

"Whatever," Hitt-Man said to her over his shoulder. "You bet not tell anyone about this, or I swear to God, I'll—Ah!" He jumped with a startle, then closed his eyes, and hissed like a snake. He trembled like he was dripping wet and standing in the middle of a meat locker. What she was doing to him felt weird at first, but then the shit started to feel good. "Awwww, fuck. You nasty, ma, for real. You a nasty, nasty bi—uhhh!" His big ole, buff ass moaned like a little ho and bit down on his bottom lip. Niqua was tongue kissing his butt-hole, massaging his nutsack, and jerking him off at the same time. All he could hear besides the shower-head's water hitting the floor was Niqua sounding like she was eating a tasty chocolate cupcake. Hearing her slobbing down his crinkle made his dick harder, and his warm semen oozed out of his pee-hole. It dropped onto the floor and swirled down the shower's drain. "Awww, shiiiiiit, ooooou, don't stop! Don't stop, babe, I'm finna bust! Yeah, the king finna bust! Suck it, suck it, suuuuck iiiiit!" His voice strained and his face balled up. The veins across his forehead, neck, arms, and back plumped. It made him look like he was struggling to bench press 300 pounds.

"Mmmmm, mmmm, mmmm!" Niqua moaned loudly with her eyes closed. Her head was moving like a chicken as she sucked on his dick and massaged his hanging nutsack. She even went as far as to shove her thumb up his asshole like he'd specifically told her not to. She was expecting some resistance, but it never came. All she got in response was him moaning louder and pressing his butt back at her. "Mmmmm, mmmmm."

"Aw, yeah, aw, yeaaah," Hitt-Man said in pleasure. His eyes were squeezed shut and he was throwing his ass back into her thumb while she sucked on him. Her wet, scorching mouth, accompanied by her massaging his balls and thumbing his butt-hole, had him on cloud nine. "I'ma bust, I'ma bust all up in yo'— all in yo' fucking mouth!"

Reaching down, Hitt-Man grabbed a fistful of Niqua's hair and spread his legs. He squatted down, and she held tight to his thighs with her eyes closed. He placed one hand against the wall and started fucking her mouth. He was dropping dick down her throat recklessly and not giving a fuck how she felt on the receiving end. His ass bounced up and down with each powerful thrust. The imprint of his long, fat ass dick could be seen going down her throat as he humped into mouth, with his nutsack smacking against her chin.

"Ack, ack, ack, gag, gag, gag, ack, ack!" Niqua's eyes were squeezed shut as her mouth was being fucked like a pussy. Saliva built up inside of her grill and spilled down her chin. Her face was balled up so tight that she looked like she was in pain. She was—a little—but she wasn't about to stop him and fuck up the nut he was chasing after. A moment later, a pinkish green slime with tiny food particles erupted from her mouth and spilled down her chest. The flowing shower water ran over her face and body, whisking the slime away down the drain.

"Aww, yes, aww, fuck!" Hitt-Man whined as he continued to pummel Niqua's throat. He squeezed his hand into a fist and the veins in it plumped. Again, the veins plumped over his forehead,

16

neck, arms, and body as well. His eyes rolled back to their white sides and his mouth hung open. He could feel the pressure in his dick from his semen building up and demanding to be released. "Awwwww, yes, here the king cums! Here—the—king— cuuuummmms—ugh, ugh, ugh, ugh, ugh!" His face balled up like he was angry as he slammed his dick down her throat repeatedly. He squared his jaws, releasing all his rich, creamy baby batter down inside her mouth. He then ground inside of her grill, gave her three more good pumps, and pulled himself out of her. A look of bliss spread across his face, and he stood upright. His eyes were still closed as he smiled. He glanced down and saw Niqua sucking his dick like she was trying to get every last drop from out of him. She popped him out of her mouth and it sounded like a suction cup. Looking up at him, she smiled and told him that she loved him.

"I love you too, queen," Hitt-Man replied, breathing huskily. He helped her to her feet and she got a washcloth wet and soapy. She directed him to turn around and face the wall. "What chu 'bouta do? Wash a nigga up?" He glanced over his shoulder at her, wearing a smirk.

"Unh huh," Niqua said, then kissed him on his cheek. She then went about the task of soaping up his body. She softly sang a love song while she performed what she believed were her wifely duties. He placed his forehead against the wall, closed his eyes, and listened to her angelic voice as she crooned. She'd always had a beautiful singing voice. He believed she could have been a wonderful singer had she chosen to pursue a music career instead of being the wife of a kingpin.

"Baby," Hitt-Man called for her attention.

"Yes, sweetheart?" Niqua answered as she washed his lower half.

"Remember what I said now."

"I know. I know. Don't tell anyone about what we did," she replied with a smirk.

"That's right," he said.

"Turn around, babe. I needa get cho front." Hitt-Man turned around and she started washing the front of him. "So, uh, baby, how was it?"

"On some real shit, ma, a nigga ain't never came as hard as that with any woman on the planet," Hitt-Man admitted. His confession made her smile. She figured now he wouldn't be trying to bring other bitchez in their bedroom since she'd put it on him so good.

"Oh, really?" she asked happily, feeling herself.

"Yep."

"So you liked it?"

"Liked it? Shit, I loved it," he replied. "What we do in the bedroom stays between you and me, though. Don't do no shit like that when we have other bitchez between our sheets."

The moment he said that, Niqua's heart broke and she became glassy eyed. She wanted to break down so bad. She finally understood that she'd never be enough for her husband, and that really fucked her up. Hitt-Man's eyes were still closed, so he couldn't see her crying and sniffling.

Niqua made up her mind when it came to Hitt-Man. She was going to continue to do what she needed to do to keep him with her. Although it would kill her inside, it was better than losing him.

Damn!

Chapter Two
Los Angeles

Arnez pulled up to the rally point and everyone jumped out the Tahoe. He ran from around the SUV, heading over to the trunk of his Chevy Impala. He needed to get the duffle bag containing their change of clothes and the gasoline can to set the G-ride ablaze. While he was occupied doing this, KiMani and Zekey were supposed to be changing out of their clothes.

Zekey sat his gun down on the hood of the Tahoe and pulled his hoodie from over his head. He then started unbuckling his belt and removing his jeans. KiMani came from around the opposite side of the SUV and cracked him in his mouth. Zekey staggered backwards, with his jeans around his ankles, and fell awkwardly to the ground. He turned over on his elbows and looked at KiMani, blinking his eyes like he'd just awoken.

"I told yo' mothafucking ass before we got there, I'm not slumping any kids, and what the fuck did you do? You killed a poor, defenseless lil' girl," KiMani barked on him.

"Yeah, you're right—I did," Zekey told him as blood slid out the corner of his mouth. He smiled devilishly and wiped his mouth. "Guess what? I'd do that lil' bitch again, if it meant I could get my hands on Travieso."

"You're a diseased dog that has to be put down—for good!" Kimani said, extending his gun to Zekey's forehead. The older man was on his hands and knees like a dog. He stared up at the youth fearlessly. He wasn't afraid of death. In fact, he welcomed it.

"Oh, yeah? And who's gonna be the one to do it?" Zekey smiled harder.

"Me!" KiMani snarled and squeezed the trigger.

"Nooooo!" Arnez screamed.

Bloc!

Arnez kicked KiMani's wrist, and his gun discharged close to Zekey's ear. Zekey clutched at the side of his head as an eerie siren wailed within his ear canal. His eyes were bulged and his lips were pursed. He fell several times trying to get back up on his feet. The overwhelming sound of the piece being fired so close to his ear had thrown off his equilibrium. When he finally did make it up on his feet, he was staggering like a drunk out of a bar. He could see Arnez and KiMani arguing and struggling over control of his gun. It appeared like the youngsta was trying to come over and pop his ass, but Arnez was trying to stop him.

Zekey pulled his jeans up and crashed to the ground. He looked to the hood of the Tahoe and spotted his gun. His face transformed to a mask of determination and hatred. His only function now was to pop KiMani for attempting to knock the noodles out of his head. It took several attempts, but Zekey finally managed to grab his blower from off the hood. He turned around, struggling to maintain his balance as well as his aim. That didn't stop him from blasting at KiMani though. The first shot went wild and wasn't nearly as close as Zekey would have liked for it to have been.

The first shot also alerted KiMani and Arnez to the fact that Zekey was strapped. Seeing Zekey was incapable of taking a decent shot, KiMani decided to take advantage of the situation.

"Fuck out my way, Blood!" KiMani shoved Arnez aside roughly. "I'ma put old head outta his misery." He ran forward and got down on one knee, lifting his gun. He angled his head and shut one of his eyes. Arnez was running towards KiMani as fast as he could, for fear of him baptizing Zekey in his own blood.

"Ki, no, stop!" Arnez said, drawing closer to him. "Unc, stop, no!"

Bloc! Bloc!

Zekey fired two more shots. One zipped dangerously close to KiMani's head while the other struck the ground, creating a dirt cloud. KiMani's eyebrows slanted and his nose wrinkled. He'd just lined up the sightings of his gun with Zekey's forehead.

Bloc!

***

The light from the television's screen danced across Lachaun's face as she tossed and turned in bed. She was trying to

20

fall asleep, but her mind was racked with thoughts of KiMani. She hadn't heard from him since he disappeared from the funeral with Arnez, and he wasn't answering his cell phone. She'd left him a million messages and hoped he'd get back with her soon. Once her jack rang, she rushed to answer it, thinking it was him, but it was Hellraiser, calling to see if she'd heard from KiMani yet.

"Nah, baby, no such luck yet," Lachaun regretfully informed him. "I'm hoping to hear from 'em soon. If I don't, then I'ma get dressed and file a missing person's report."

"Okay, baby," Hellraiser said. "I know KiMani isn't technically your son, but I—"

"Nuh, unh." She shook her head. "You stop right there. You're right, Ki, isn't my son. He's our son. I'll never look at 'em any different than I will when I have this one I'm lugging along now," she assured him as she rubbed her belly lovingly. A smile etched across her lips thinking of their family being complete once she'd given birth to their little prince and her husband was finally home.

"One million, nine hundred and forty-six thousand."

"What's that, babe?"

"Just adding one more to the total of reasons I love you."

"Awwww, honey, you're so sweet," Lachaun said, blushing like a high school girl with a crush.

"I know, right? You gon' mess around and get diabetes fucking with me."

Lachaun threw her head back, laughing. "Oh my God, Treymaine, that was so corny!"

"Aye, it got chu laughing though, lil' mama."

She came down from her laughter saying, "True, true, true."

Lachaun and Hellraiser talked for one more hour before she disconnected the call to file the missing person's report. She threw on some pajamas, her bomber jacket with the fur around the hood, and grabbed her purse and her .357 magnum revolver. She made the report and stopped at 7-11 to grab a slurpy. Afterwards, she came home and slipped on her gown for bed. She tried her best, but no matter what, she couldn't fall asleep.

Lachaun's eyes peeled open, and she rolled over onto her back and stared up at the ceiling. She couldn't sleep, and on top of that, she had to piss. It seemed like ever since she'd gotten knocked up, she'd been running back and forth to the bathroom, every ten minutes or so. Her bladder was giving her so much hell she was afraid of taking so much as a sip of water. She felt like if she did, then she'd spend most of the night in the bathroom.

"Damn, slurpy," Lachaun thought aloud as she grabbed her cellphone from the nightstand. She waddled like a duck down the hallway, rubbing her round belly with one hand, and searching her contacts with the other.

"Ooooh, shit, lemme hurry up 'fore this shit spill down my legs," Lachaun said. She dropped the hand she held her cell phone in at her side and sped up her waddling. Bursting open the bathroom door, she quickly slid down her panties and plopped down on the toilet seat. Lachaun threw her head back, and a look of satisfaction overcame her face as she relieved her bladder. She hit up KiMani and listened to the ringing as she studied her nails. The new growth was pushing the fake nails up from their roots. "I needa get my shit done—ASAP."

A rap on the bathroom window startled Lachaun and made her drop her cellular. As she picked it up, she could hear another jack ringing outside the window. She wiped herself, flushed the toilet, and answered her jack.

"Hello?" Lachaun said into the cell phone, peering out of the window.

"Chaun, it's me, open the door for me," KiMani replied.

"Boy, you scared the living shit outta me," Lachaun told him.

"My bad. I didn't mean to, but you weren't answering the front door."

"It's okay, baby. I've gotta get chu a key since you're gonna be staying here from now on."

"Smooth. I'm finna go around to the front door."

"Alright." He disconnected the call and disappeared inside of the bushes.

Lachaun waddled to the front door and opened it, stepping aside. As KiMani crossed the threshold, she noticed the soulless look in his eyes. It was the same look his father had when he'd killed someone. Her theory was confirmed when she saw the smudges of dirt on his sneakers and dots of blood on them. He'd definitely taken someone's life. Well, technically, he'd taken a few lives that particular night.

Lachaun locked the door behind KiMani. She then cupped his face and looked into his eyes. He was quiet and withdrawn, so she wondered if he had ever killed someone before.

"Was tonight your first time?" Lachaun asked him. He gave her a look that let her know tonight wasn't his first time laying something down. "Okay, all right." She nodded understandingly. "Well, let's get chu outta those clothes and sneakers so you can take a bath. I needa wash your hair and put 'em inna few braids. How'd you like that?" she asked as she played with the frizzes of his cornrows.

"Smooth." He nodded nonchalantly.

"Did you get rid of it?" she asked him about the gun he'd used in the murders. He nodded. "Good." She cupped his face again, kissing him on both cheeks and then his forehead. "Okay, sweetie, you go ahead and take off those clothes while I draw you a bath." She caressed the side of his face and kissed him again. "Boy, if you don't look like yo' daddy." He flashed her a weak smile and she went to draw him a tub of water.

KiMani stripped down to his boxer briefs and left his clothes in a pile at his bare feet. Lachaun returned with a comb, which she left on the living room table. She gathered KiMani's pile of clothes and tossed them into the fireplace.

"Those aren't the clothes I wore tonight," KiMani said flatly.

"I hear you, sweetie, but I think it's best I get rid of them—just to be on the safe side, ya know?" With that said, Lachaun squirted his clothing with lighter fluid, struck a match, and tossed it on top of the clothes.

Frooosh!

The clothes and sneakers erupted into flames and Lachaun jumped back, screaming. She laughed and looked back at KiMani. He appeared to be lost in his thoughts. He was staring ahead but not looking at her. Lachaun dropped the smile from her face and looked back at the flames. The golden light of the fire shone on her face.

"Well, we've gotten rid of that," Lachaun said of the clothes burning in the fireplace.

Lachaun turned off the water flowing into the tub. She returned to the living room and took down KiMani's hair. She then combed it out and led him into the bathroom. She gave him her back and allowed him to privately strip naked. KiMani dipped his hand into the water and found it to be to his satisfaction. He stepped into the water and sat down.

"You in?" Lachaun inquired with her back turned.

"Yeah."

Lachaun gathered the shampoo and conditioner bottles and sat them beside the tub. She could tell that KiMani wasn't in the right state of mind to wash himself up, so she asked him if it was okay if she did. He nodded yes. Lachaun took her time to lather KiMani up and rinse him off. She then shampooed and conditioned his hair. As she massaged the conditioner into his scalp, she sang Boys II Men's "A Song for Mama." Ironically, it was the same song that was played at Big Ma's funeral. Unbeknownst to her, KiMani's eyes turned pink and quickly filled with water. He shut his eyes and tears jetted down his cheeks. He bowed his head and his body slowly began to shiver.

You were there for me to love and care for me
When skies were gray
Whenever I was down
You were always there to—

Feeling KiMani shivering, Lachaun became concerned, and she abruptly stopped conditioning his hair.

"What's wrong, baby?" Lachaun asked with worry in her tone. She slid around to the front of KiMani and tilted his chin up. His eyes were shut, but when he peeled them open, the tears seemed like they were never going to stop. "Awe, sweetie, what's the matter?"

Lachaun continued to probe him, but he wouldn't answer her. So she set the comb aside and hugged him to her. She lay the side of her face against his thick crop of conditioned hair and shut her eyes. He closed his eyes and leaned into her. He shivered harder and that made her worry about him.

"Hug me tighter," KiMani told her, his voice cracking emotionally.

Lachaun obliged him and kissed him on the side of his face. She began humming a happy and comforting song that caused him to sob. His body shivered and he held her tighter. She allowed him to weep as she rubbed his back motherly.

Lachaun held onto KiMani a while longer. When she went to pull away, he held her in place, never wanting her to let go. She grinned, kissed him again, and started back humming the comforting tune again.

Twenty minutes later

KiMani dried off and got dressed in the underwear Lachaun left out for him. He brushed his teeth as he stared at his reflection in the medicine cabinet mirror. His mind took him back to what happened hours prior.

***

"Ki, no, stop!" Arnez said, drawing closer to him. "Unc, stop! No!"

Bloc! Bloc!

Zekey fired two more shots. One zipped dangerously close to KiMani's head while the other struck the ground, creating a dirt cloud. KiMani's eyebrows slanted and his nose wrinkled. He'd just lined the sightings of his gun up with Zekey's forehead.

Bloc!

Arnez tackled KiMani from behind as he pulled the trigger of his gun. An empty shell casing disengaged from the side of his piece, and a hollow-tip bullet rocketed out of its barrel. Sparks

25

flew out behind the flat-head bullet, as it ripped through the air like a missile. The bullet was quickly closing the distance between itself and Zekey. The older man fired his gun again, and another dirt cloud materialized near Arnez and KiMani. Zekey was still staggering like a drunk. All of his wobbling caused the bullet intended to knock his wig off to pierce the side of his shoulder. His face balled up in pain as fire ignited in his shoulder. He grasped his wound and hurled back to the ground. He looked at his fingers and they came away bloody. The next thing he knew, the ground was coming up to meet him.

Wam!

"Gaaaah, fuck!" Zekey cussed, feeling the burning sensation in his shoulder. When he looked ahead, he saw Arnez snatching KiMani's gun away from him and pulling him up to his feet. KiMani mad dogged him as he brushed the dirt from his jeans.

"Unc, Unc, are you all right, man?" a worried Arnez asked as he ran toward him, tucking KiMani's piece into the small of his back. He got down on his knees where Zekey had fallen and examined his wound. "You'll be straight, the bullet just grazed you. Come on." He grabbed his gun from the ground and helped Zekey to his feet. The older man saw through a haze of red. He was as mad as a bull and wanted a piece of KiMani's ass.

Zekey's equilibrium was a little off, but he was sure he'd have better luck painting KiMani's ass bloody.

"Gemme my shit, nephew, I'm 'bout to splash this young ass nigga!" Zekey mad dogged KiMani from where he was changing out of his clothes at the trunk of Arnez's whip.

KiMani was keeping an eye on Zekey as he slipped into his fresh set of clothes. Before he unzipped the duffle bag that had his change of gear in it, he discreetly withdrew the tire arm from out of the spare tire compartment. He didn't have a gun, and Arnez had disarmed Zekey. So he wasn't sweating getting popped. If push came to shove, they'd take a head-up fade, but it sure as hell wasn't going to be a fair one. Zekey's big swole ass was four or five times bigger than him. He'd split his shit to the white meat with the tire iron before he saw him from the shoulders.

"Nah, Unc, it ain't gon' be alla that," Arnez told him. *"That's my brother right there. I love 'em to death, for real, for real."*

"So, what chu saying, nephew? You choosing this lil' nigga over me?" Zekey looked at him in disbelief. He was low-key shocked! *"You love this fool more than you love ya boy? A nigga that taught chu the streets, and raised you from a pup to a big dog?"*

Arnez looked away and took a deep breath. Bowing his head, he massaged his temples and then looked back up at Zekey. *"Yo, I love both of y'all niggaz equally. I don't hold either of you above the other. Y'all my fam. That's why I can't have y'all tryna off one another! Straight up!"* Zekey thought of where Arnez was coming from and nodded his understanding.

"I'm outta here, my nigga. Deuces!" KiMani said as he turned to walk away, throwing up two fingers.

"Yo, Ki, hol' up, man, I'ma drop you off," Arnez called out to him, but he kept on walking like he didn't hear him. *"Kiiii!"* he waited for him to respond, but he kept on walking. *"Kiiiii!"*

"Fuck that nigga, Blood. Let's soak this ride and get the fuck outta here," Zekey told Arnez as he walked back over to him. He was in a fresh pair of clothes and carrying a red gasoline can.

"Damn," Arnez said in disappointment. He watched KiMani's back as he walked away for a minute, before dipping off to help Zekey. They placed their murder gear and sneakers inside of the Tahoe. They then soaked them and the rest of the SUV.

Arnez swung his Chevy Impala around so it would be facing the direction that KiMani was walking. He placed the last of the guns they'd used in the hit in a leather, peanut butter-brown bag and zipped it up. When he set it on the passenger side floor, he lifted his head back up to see Zekey tossing a struck match inside the Tahoe.

Froosh!

Zekey took off running towards Arnez's Chevy. He snatched the door opened and hopped inside. As soon as he slammed the door shut, the car took off like a bat out of hell.

***

KiMani would have blown Zekey's head off, but Arnez intervened. He knew firsthand how Zekey got down when he was beefing with a nigga. The dopehead was a straight-up killa. So, he was sure whenever they bumped into each other again, it was going to be on. Only one person would come out as the victor, and he was going to make damn sure it was him. That's exactly why the first thing tomorrow morning, he was going to make a couple of calls to see about getting himself a new gun. He wasn't trying to be caught slipping without one, especially now since he'd clashed with a killa the streets respected immensely.

KiMani finished brushing his teeth, washed his mouth out, and gargled with Listerine. He then wiped his mouth with a towel hanging from the rack and left the bathroom. He was making his way down the hallway when Lachaun call for him.

"Yeah," KiMani asked as soon as he appeared in the doorway of her bedroom. She was lying on her side underneath the covers, and the light cast from the TV was shone on her.

"I can't seem to fall asleep," Lachaun told him. "I think it's 'cause I'm so used to yo' father lying beside me. You mind keeping me company in bed? Just for the night?" She looked at him with pleading eyes, hoping he'd say yes. KiMani didn't know she was lying her ass off! Lachaun wanted him to sleep with her tonight so she could comfort him. She knew he was still hurting from the passing of his grandmother and the incarceration of his father. She desperately wanted to love on him and help him heal. She truly adored KiMani and wanted to be there for him.

"Only on one condition."

"What's that?"

"You lemme hold that .357 you keep in yo' purse."

Lachaun grinned. She didn't have any idea that he knew she stayed strapped. "I tell you what, if you agree to tell me what chu needa blower for, then I'll let chu hold my baby down. Deal?" she asked as she extended her delicate hand.

KiMani looked at her lingering hand and then up into Lachaun's eyes. She was ride or die for his father, and he knew that she was privy to a lot of his business. On top of that, she was from the same hood as him and his old man. It wasn't like she was some square-ass bitch! She was a down-ass homegirl!

"Okay," KiMani said and shook her hand. He then sat on the side of the bed and told her about the beef he had with Zekey. He didn't leave anything out, besides Arnez's involvement. "So, yeah, now I gotta keep a piece on me at all times. I'll never know when I'ma bump into this fool, you feel me?"

Lachaun nodded and said, "What makes you think he'll come here?"

"To my knowledge, he doesn't know about yo' crib. Really, me being able to sleep witcho blower tonight will just make me feel better."

"Okay, a deals a deal," Lachaun told him. Although most adults would never give a child a loaded gun, KiMani was far from your average child. He was wise beyond his years, and he knew the streets like the back of his hand. She already knew he was in the trenches dropping bodies, so she felt like he was responsible enough to hold her pistol down.

Lachaun opened her nightstand drawer and removed her .357 magnum revolver. She already knew it was fully loaded but she checked the chamber again out of habit. She closed the chamber of the revolver and handed it to KiMani. She watched from the bed as he examined the piece of steel. He shut one eye, lifted the weapon, and aimed it at different items in the bedroom.

"This a nice piece, Mo—" KiMani's eyes doubled in size and he smacked his hand over his mouth. He nearly called Lachaun "momma." He felt embarrassed and wished he could have vanished into an explosion of smoke. Unfortunately for him, he couldn't. "My bad, Chaun, I didn't mean t—"

"It's okay, sweetie," Lachaun assured him as she took him by his hand, leading him over into the bed. She had him lay with his back to her and she snuggled up behind him, placing her hand on his shoulder. "You can call me momma if you want. It would be an honor. Can I call you son?" she asked with a smile. When she heard him nearly call her momma, it made her feel warm and fuzzy inside. She'd always loved KiMani like he was her flesh and blood. She'd be proud for him to call her mom or momma, or whatever he chose.

"Y—yeah," KiMani said hesitantly.

"Good," she said happily as she rubbed her fingers through his wild hair. She was supposed to put it in six cornrows, but he didn't feel like getting it done right then. So, they agreed she'd do his hair after they ate breakfast tomorrow morning.

"Momma…"

"Yes, son?"

"You mind putting your arm around me and humming to me like you did when I was in the tub?"

"No problem, sweetie, momma got chu faded," Lachaun assured him as she snaked her arm around him. She brushed his wild hair with her hand while humming to him. The soft humming by his ear put him at ease. He closed his eyes and his hand loosened from around the handle of the revolver.

Lachaun continued to hum and gently brush KiMani's hair with her hand. Five minutes passed by before she eventually called KiMani's name to make sure he was asleep. He didn't respond! Reaching over him, she took the .357 from his hand and placed it back into the top nightstand drawer. She closed it back and snuggled up behind KiMani again. Shutting her eyes, she held him with one hand and brushed his hair with the other.

"I love you, son," she said in a hushed tone.

KiMani made a face and squirmed around a little.

"I love you too, momma," he replied, getting comfortable to go back to sleep.

Lachaun smiled broadly and kissed him on his temple. She continued to comfort him until she eventually fell asleep.

Chapter Three
Night

"KiMani, what's the matter? What's going on?" Hellraiser asked his son as he paced the floor, contraband cellular held to his ear. His heart was thudding like crazy, fearing the worst outcome for his newborn son.

"Pops, he's not—he's not breathing," KiMani said in a panic.

"Oh my God, no!" Hellraiser heard Lachaun in the background.

Hearing that his baby boy wasn't breathing caused Hellraiser's heart to skip a beat, and his eyes doubled in size. His right knee buckled and he slowly kneeled to the floor. He felt faint and nauseated.

This is it! I know what this is! This is karma coming back to me for all the fucked up shit I've done while I was in the streets. First, I lost my baby's mama, I got sent to the pen, lost my oldest son to the streets, then had my mother taken away from me. Fuck, blood! I know a nigga been living foul, but, damn, to punish me for my sins like this, though. I'd rather you take me, Lord. Take me instead of my lil' man, Hellraiser thought as his eyes turned glassy and tears slowly accumulated in them.

"What's the doctor and the nurses doing now?"

"They're tryna revive 'em, they're tryna revive the baby."

"Okay. Great, listen, son, I want chu to tend to Lachaun. Comfort her, hold her hand for me, okay?"

"Yeah, Pops, I got chu," he responded. "I got chu, ma. Everything is gonna be straight. Let's pray, okay? Matter fact, Pops, you too, all right? We'll pray together."

"I'm witchu, son, I'm here."

Hellraiser could hear Lachaun crying in the background, but he could tell she was trying to pull herself together.

"Alright, I'ma lead the prayer," KiMani began, clearing his throat before proceeding. "Dear God, my family and I come to you today to ask that you spare my baby brother, Billion. He just entered this world, Father. So please, please, give 'em a chance at a life…" KiMani continued on with his prayer, but unbeknownst to him, his father had muted the cell phone and was on his knees citing a prayer of his own.

Hellraiser had his fingers interlocked and was staring up at the ceiling. As quickly as his eyes would fill up with tears, they'd jet down his cheeks. "God, I ask that you please allow my infant son to live. He's just a baby, and he hasn't gotten a chance to experience life yet. I know I've done some horrible things in my lifetime and this may be your way of punishing me. But I beg of you, don't handle things like this—don't do it this way. Don't use my boy as a pawn to get back at m—" Feeling a hand grasp his shoulder, he turned his head and found OG standing at his rear. He hadn't heard the old man climb down from his bed. He gathered he must have been so focused on the task at hand that he'd neglected everything else going on around him.

"I'm here, son, this is our family. I got cha back," OG told him. "Go ahead—continue," he urged him. He then shut his eyes and bowed his head.

Hellraiser turned back around and continued to cite his prayer. "Father, I throw myself at your feet and plead for mercy. I swear that if you spare my child's life that I'll renounce violence in any form. I vow to change my life for the good! I swear on it! If I am lying, may you strike me dead with a bolt of lightning! Amen!" When Hellraiser finished his prayer, his face was soaked and snot was creeping out of his right nostril. Shortly thereafter, his contraband cell phone vibrated and its display lit up. It glowed in the darkness. Picking it up, he looked at the screen and saw "KiMani." He climbed to his feet and looked up at his father. "It's Ki, Pops. I think he may have hung up 'cause I wasn't responding during the prayer. I bet he has an update about the baby."

"You won't know until you answer the call, son," OG told him and placed his hands on his shoulders. The cell phone stopped vibrating. Hellraiser looked down at its display and a missed call was on it. Abruptly, its display lit up as it started vibrating again.

Hellraiser's heart was thudding loud and hard. He could hear it inside of his ears. He was fearful of what KiMani was going to tell him. He wondered if God had answered his prayer.

"I know you're afraid, but eventually, you're gonna have to deal with the situation, son." OG gave him the truth raw and uncut, like a kilo of cocaine from Bogotá, Colombia. "Besides, your wife is gonna need your help getting through this."

Hellraiser nodded understandingly and said, "You're right, Pops." He answered the call and KiMani's voice boomed through his cellular's speakers.

"Pops! Pops! They saved 'em, they saved 'em! He's alive, he's alive!" KiMani said excitedly.

"Waa, waa, waa, waa, waaaa!" Hellraiser could hear baby Billion's hollering in the background. This confirmed that he was alive and well.

Instantly, Hellraiser's eyes lit up and his mouth hung open. He looked up at his father with tears of joy dancing in his eyes. "It's okay! He's okay! My baby boy's okay!" He hugged his father tightly. OG kissed his cheek and they jumped up and down joyfully.

"Baby—baby, are you there?" Lachaun's voice resonated through the cell phone. You could tell by the sound of her voice that she was emotional and had been crying.

Hellraiser turned from OG and placed his cell to his ear. "Yes, babe, I'm here."

"Oh, I love you! I love you so much!" Lachaun told him tearfully. Her voice cracked with emotion.

"Here goes your son, Mrs. James," Hellraiser heard a feminine voice tell his wife. He didn't know it, but baby Billion had his umbilical cord snipped. He'd also been bathed, diapered, and wrapped snug in a blanket KiMani had bought him from the store downstairs.

"Babe, which one of us does he look like?" Hellraiser asked excitedly. OG was standing beside him waiting in anticipation of Lachaun's answer.

"Oh my God, he's beautiful, baby. He's the most beautiful baby in the world," she swore happily. "He looks like, I'd say he looks like—"

"Grandpa!" KiMani blurted.

"That's exactly right. He looks a lot like your father, but I can also see some of me in his features too."

"Pops, she says he looks like you," Hellraiser told his old man.

"Oh, really? Mannn, I can't wait to see a picture of my grandson." OG smiled and hung his arm around Hellraiser's shoulders.

Hellraiser and Lachaun went on talking throughout the night. He eventually told her the vow he made to God. She told him that it was time he made a change anyway for the sake of his family. He agreed. OG talked to Lachaun for a while and she sent him a few pictures of the baby. The old head was smiling in amazement of how much his grandson looked like him. He couldn't take his eyes off the pictures. He made Lachaun promise to send him physical pictures of baby Billion so he could hang them on the wall of his cell. Afterward, he shot the shit with KiMani since he hadn't talked to him for a while. They laughed and joked before OG started preaching to him about leaving the streets alone. KiMani listened respectfully but eventually terminated the conversation.

"Alright, Grandpa, I gotta take a leak. I'ma holla at chu later," KiMani told him. It was then that OG knew that what he said went in one ear and out of the other. The young nigga wasn't trying to hear that shit he was talking about.

"Okay then, grandson, I love you too," OG replied.

"Pops, tell Lachaun I'ma call her tomorrow," Hellraiser told his father from the bottom bunk. His fingers were interlocked behind his head and he appeared to be wrapped in his thoughts.

OG relayed the message to KiMani, who then told Lachaun what his father had said. Afterward, the old head disconnected the call and passed it to Hellraiser. He decided to charge it up so he could use it for tomorrow when he hollered at Lachaun.

OG had just lay back in his bunk and shut his eyes when Hellraiser started back talking to him.

"Pops!"

OG took an exhausted breath. It wasn't because he didn't feel like talking. It was because he was genuinely sleepy and wanted to take his old ass to bed.

"What's up, son?" he asked, peeling his eyes back open.

"I'm out."

"Yeah, I know. I heard you make that deal with the Man upstairs."

"Not just with being your muscle, but with everything, Pops," Hellraiser told him. "I mean, I'm done with gangbanging too. In here and out there, I'm distancing myself from this shit—for real, for real. I made a vow to The Big Man and I've gotta keep it for the sake of my family."

"Understood," OG replied. "You know I'm holding the keys to the yard, so you've got my blessing. As far as my business is concerned"—he took a deep breath—"I'll have the youngin' hold me down."

"Who?" Hellraiser inquired with a curious frown.

"You know, the youngin'," OG said, snapping his fingers as he tried to recall the young goon's name. "Umm, umm, damn, why can't I recall this kid's name? I rap with 'em every day."

"Uhhh, Kyjuan?" he threw a name out there, hoping it stuck with his pops.

"Yeah, that's him." OG smiled as he thought about the youth and his get-down. "I really fucks with new blood. Lil' homie reminds me of myself coming up. He's young, heartless, and doesn't give a fuck."

"It's his not giving a fuck that landed his young ass in here for the long haul."

OG smiled harder and said, "Now, son, are you jealous?"

Hellraiser and OG laughed heartily.

"Nah, I'm not jelly, old man." He continued to laugh before they both became silent. "But on some real shit, Pops, thanks."

"No thanks needed. We do what we gotta do to take care of family—our family."

"Fa sho'."

"Now, do yo' old man a favor, and shut the fuck up, alright? I need my beauty sleep."

Hellraiser smiled and shut his eyes. His father pulled his blanket over him and adjusted himself on his bunk. He then shut his eyes for a good night's rest.

***

2015
Daylight

Blat!

A young man's head ricocheted off the pavement. His red Cardinals baseball cap landed beside him. It had a singed hole on the side of it and it was smoking. The side of his head was missing and he was bleeding profusely. His eyes were wide with shock and his mouth was stretched so far open you could see every tooth in his mouth. He was dead!

"They got 'em, they got Lil' D, Blood!" Papoose called out to Assassin, having seen their comrade meet his end. The young men were headed to Venice Beach to play basketball and take in the sights when they spotted some fine ass women in skimpy clothes. They pulled over and flagged the girls down. They were in the middle of spitting G when a gunman hanging out of the window of a Dodge Charger started spraying shit up. They were forced to abandon their whip and flee for their lives.

"We'll mourn our loss later, Blood! Keep moving!" Assassin told him as he continued to run with a gun in each of his hands. He was a dark-skinned nigga who wore his shoulder-length hair in locs. He had a bull's-eye inked on his forehead and red teardrops at either corner of his eyes. The young man was a week shy of his twenty-third birthday and was nearing a body count his same age. He'd made his bones dropping opps and taking hits for cold cash like his father before him.

"Alright," Papoose replied, as he continued to run at his side. He was strapped right alongside Assassin. Their pistols weren't hitting on shit against that big ass Uzi the shooter was getting at them with. That mothafucka sounded like a typewriter!

Blatatatatatatatatatat!

Papoose and Assassin huffed and puffed as they bent the corner of the next block. They were running as fast as they could, sweat sliding down their faces, shirts clinging to them due to their heavy perspiration. They were hot, sticky, and tired as hell, but they had to keep moving if they were going to live to see another day.

Urrrrrk!

The sound of tires squealing could be heard at the end of the block, where Papoose and Assassin had bent the corner running from. Following behind them, was a royal blue 2015 Dodge Charger SRT Hellcat with two black racing stripes. It had been in hot pursuit of them. Its driver had nearly lost control of the vehicle and crashed it. The vehicle was in a hurry to catch up with them. The shooter was eager to claim their lives. The car was in the background as the young men ran for their lives, but it was quickly closing the distance between them.

Blatatatatatatatatatat!

A nineteen-year-old KiMani hung halfway out the back window of the Charger. He had his black submachine Uzi pointed in Papoose and Assassin's direction, spitting hot flames at them. The automatic weapon jerked violently as it spat quick bursts of fire, sending empty shell casings flying from the side of it. The young nigga wore a red "T" baseball cap low over his brows, black sunglasses, and a red bandana over the lower half of his face. He boasted the perfect disguise. The only one that knew who he was besides his right-hand man, Arnez, was God Almighty.

"You hit 'em yet? You hit 'em?" Arnez asked from behind the wheel of the stolen Dodge Charger. He wore the same disguise as his comrade, except his baseball cap was backwards.

"I got Lil' D's bitch ass, but I missed Papoose and Assassin!" KiMani announced to his main man. He watched as Papoose and Assassin continued to flee up the street. "Floor this bitch, Blood! We can't let these ho-ass niggaz getta way! Get me close enough to cut 'em both down!"

"I got chu faded." He gave him a nod and punched out, mashing the gas pedal further. The red hand on the speedometer swept around the circle. The Charger blew past the cars and houses aligning both sides of the block. The vehicle neared the right side of the street heading towards the corner Assassin and Papoose had just turned running.

Urrrrrrrk!

Arnez made a tight turn that nearly flipped the Charger over, leaving it on three wheels for a second before it came back down on the black top. He mashed the brake pedal a little as he bent the corner of the next block. Arnez mashed the gas pedal again, and the red hand hastily made its way around the speedometer.

Vrooom!

Woop! Woop! Woop! Woop!

The air surrounding the car sounded as it flew down the street. It passed several cars and houses, making them look like blurs on either side of the sports car. Papoose glanced over his shoulder again while running. He took an awkward step and fell forward, colliding with the sidewalk. The impact sent his gun spinning in circles as it slid across the ground, falling off the curb. Grimacing, Papoose looked at his rear and saw the Charger coming up fast. KiMani was now sitting on the windowsill, gripping his Uzi with both hands, eyes zeroed in on him.

"Assassin, hold up!" Papoose called out to his main man, watching his back as he ran away. He was in the process of getting up from where he'd fallen.

Hearing his homeboy in distress, Assassin glanced over his shoulder and saw him scrambling to his feet. He also took note that KiMani was preparing to wet his ass up. The thought of his homeboy's life being in danger, enraged him. Gripping both of his bangaz, he slowed down and whipped around. Both blowers aimed at the speeding Charger sideways, he pulled their triggers consecutively.

"You want some, then come get some! Gang, gang, niggaz!" Assassin spat with furious eyes while biting down on his bottom lip. His guns danced in his hands as their barrels spat fire back to back. They sounded like thunderous rumbling of dark clouds right before lightning flashed and rain poured.

Blocka, blocka, blocka, blocka, blocka!

Assassin, narrowing his eyes and biting down harder on his bottom lip, walked forward, sending heat through the windshield of the Charger. The sports car jerked to the right as the driver lost control of it. KiMani fell out of the window, and the car slammed into the back of a big ass F-150. Upon impact, the front of the Charger burst into flames. Its windshield cracked into a spider's cobweb.

"Punk-ass mothafuckaz," Assassin said, mad dogging the burning Charger and lowering his smoking guns. Hearing an approaching police car siren, he looked up the block and saw Papoose finally getting up on his feet. He dusted off his pants and looked around for his banga. He found it and tucked it at the small of his back. Assassin followed suit and tucked his blowers at the front of his jeans. "Come on, Blood, we've gotta move. The boyz onna way." He tapped Papoose and they sprinted up the sidewalk, ducking off inside an alleyway.

"Uhhh!" KiMani groaned, feeling a migraine coming on from his falling out the Charger into the street. He peeled his head up from the asphalt and discovered one of the lenses of his sunglasses was cracked into a cobweb. He saw double watching Assassin and Papoose running up the sidewalk. "Niggaz think they're 'bouta getta way, unh unh!"

KiMani scowled and scrambled to his Chuck Taylors, searching the ground for his Uzi. As soon as he recovered it, he checked its magazine and smacked it back inside of its handle. *Click-Clack!* He cocked it. He could hear the police car sirens heading to his location, but he figured he had enough time to body the opposition.

Gripping his Uzi with both hands, KiMani went to go after his opps, but the shrill of his best friend caught his attention. He frowned behind his disguise, wondering what was up. He was so focused on the mission he'd forgotten about Arnez. When he turned around, he saw him jerking back and forth behind the black tinted windshield of the wrecked Charger. He was hollering and trying to unbuckle his safety belt.

"Ahhhh, fuck, Blood, help me! Help me out this mothafuckaaa! Awww, shiiit!" Arnez screamed and hollered, trying desperately to get free. One of his arms was on fire now, and so was the windshield of the Charger. At this time, the police car sirens were closing in fast.

KiMani looked back and forth between Arnez burning inside of the wrecked Charger and Assassin and Papoose, who'd just disappeared inside of an alley. They were so close to splashing their asses he could taste their blood on his tongue.

Fuck it, Blood, I'll get them niggaz next time, KiMani thought as he ran toward the wrecked Charger, jumping up on the hood of it and running across it. He jumped down onto the sidewalk and used the butt of his Uzi to smash in the driver's window. It took four good whacks against the window before the glass gave. As soon as it did, KiMani tossed his Uzi aside and reached inside of the broken window. He unlocked the door from the inside and yanked it open. Seeing Arnez moving around crazily, he pulled a Swiss Army knife from his back pocket, opened it, and used it to slice the strap of the safety belt off him. Right after, he grabbed his homeboy and pulled him forward with all of his might. As soon as they collided with the sidewalk, the Charger went up in a fireball and black smoke.

Ka-Boom!

Broken tinted glass and wreckage went flying everywhere. Arm still ablaze, Arnez jumped to his feet and quickly unzipped his jacket. He snatched it off of his arm and threw it on the floor, stomping out its flame.

"You okay?" KiMani asked with concern as he approached Arnez. He was wincing and looking at his injured arm. KiMani barely touched it and Arnez hissed like a King Cobra snake, rattling its tail. His arm was smoking and its skin looked exactly like beef jerky.

"Hell naw, Blood, this shit killing me," Arnez said as he studied his wounded arm.

"We'll take care of it later, but right now, we've gotta get the fuck from outta here before twelve shows up. Come on." KiMani tapped him and picked his Uzi back up. The two of them took off running, occasionally glancing over their shoulders. They dashed up the block and ducked into the yard of a boarded-up house with tall, weeded grass. No sooner than they did, three police cars pulled up, with their red and blue sirens blaring madly.

KiMani and Arnez huffed and puffed as they made hurried footsteps through the yard of the boarded-up house. They scaled the fence into the backyard and made their way through tall yellow grass and weeds. KiMani tripped and fell, but Arnez helped him back to his feet. They continued their sprint, hearing a police helicopter approaching. They glanced up into the air and saw it coming from afar.

"Come on, nigga, we've gotta keep moving!" KiMani called out to his road dog. It was hot as fuck that day, so they were sweating underneath their disguises and clothing. KiMani tossed his Uzi into the tall, weeded grass as Arnez ran past him. He leaped forward, grabbed the top of the brick wall in front of him that separated both homes and pulled himself upon it. He sat on top of it like it was the saddle of a horse.

"Come on, Blood!" Arnez motioned for KiMani and extended his hand, flexing his fingers. KiMani charged forward, grabbed his hand, and pressed his sneaker against the brick wall. "Grrrrr!" Arnez's face balled up behind the red bandanas covering his face as he pulled his homeboy up. Once KiMani had made it up on the brick wall, they jumped down into the next yard and continued to run. Hearing a dog barking and coming at them from their left, they looked and found a big ass Rottweiler. His eyes were glinting evilly while his mouth was salivating with hunger. "Oh, shit!" Arnez's eyes bulged when he saw the angry beast. He kicked the shit out of him, and the dog yelped. The hound then turned around and chomped down on his leg. "Ahhh, fuck, Ki, get this dog, man, get this mothafucking dog!" he hollered over and over again, kicking at the Rottweiler with his free leg and punching its head.

"Grrrrrrr!" The Rottweiler shook its enormous head from left to right wildly, trying its best to tear Arnez's leg from its socket. "Grrrrr, grrrrrr, grrrrrr!"

"Mothafucking punk-ass dog, get off my homeboy! Get the fuck off of 'em!" KiMani shouted angrily as he kicked the dog as hard as he could, over and over again. No matter how brutally he assaulted the vicious animal, it wouldn't break its hold. Remembering he had his Swiss Army knife on him, KiMani pulled it out of his back pocket and opened it. A small rainbow reflected once the rays of the sun captured its blade. Grunting, he jabbed the Rottweiler in its eyes and it howled in pain, retreating. "Come on, Blood!" KiMani extended his hand to his fallen comrade and he took hold of it. He pulled him to his feet and they continued to run.

"Hey, hey, what the fuck did y'all do to my fucking dog, man!" A fat nigga with a hairy chest came bursting out of the backdoor of the house's backyard they were in. He was wearing a doo-rag, wife beater, and sweatpants. His meaty hands held tight to a big ass shotgun. It was all black with a long barrel. "Yeah, two guys wearing red bandanas just ran through my yard and assaulted my gotdamn dog! I don't know if they tryna break into my house or what, but they're on my property!" the fat nigga hollered out to the 9-1-1 operator in his Bluetooth headset secured on his ear. Spit flew out of his mouth and some of it clung to his beard, hanging from it. "It don't even matter, send the cops and tell 'em to bring two body bags!" He lifted his shotgun and went to point it at KiMani and Arnez as they climbed the gate that led to his driveway.

Bloom!

Sparks flew off the gate just as KiMani jumped down.

"Oh, fuck! Come on, man!" KiMani called out to Arnez, who was just about to hop down from the gate.

"I gotcho ass now, sucka," the fat nigga said as he trained his shotgun on Arnez. He pulled its trigger and its barrel exploded. He was too late, though, because Arnez had just jumped down to the ground and out of the way of the threat of the deadly blast. "Son of a bitch, I almost got 'em!" the fat nigga complained as he lowered his shotgun and hurried down the short steps in his house shoes. He dug inside of his pocket and pulled out a key, unlocking the gate. With one swift motion, he kicked the double gates at their center, and they flew open at once. He saw KiMani and Arnez hauling ass down his driveway. He lifted his shotgun and fired at them as they became big ass dots before his eyes. "Punk asses must have the light of Heaven shining down on their black asses, 'cause ain't no way I shoulda missed," he said, lowering his shotgun and kicking the gate angrily.

***

Assassin and Papoose huffed and puffed as they ran down the alleyway. They were hot and sticky underneath their clothes, and their faces were covered in beads of sweat. They occasionally glanced over their shoulders to see if the police were pursuing them. Though they could hear their sirens somewhere within the area, they weren't on their trail. Assassin and Papoose stopped running once they reached the end of the alley. They bent over with their hands on their knees, panting, out of breath.

"I gotta get rid of these guns in case The Ones catch up with us," Assassin said to no one particular. He then pulled out both of his guns and began wiping his fingerprints off of them. "Yo, watch my back, my nigga," he told Papoose. The young nigga nodded, wiped his sweaty face, and posted up at the end of the alley. He kept a close eye on things as Assassin finished wiping his guns clean and tossed them inside of a green trash bin overflowing with black garbage bags.

Assassin tapped Papoose's arm and he walked out of the alleyway. They made their way down the sidewalk, taking the occasional glance over their shoulders and wiping their sweaty faces.

"Aw, fuck!" Papoose said under his breath.

"What?" Assassin looked at him, wondering what was up.

"One time." Papoose nodded ahead. When Papoose looked, sure enough, a police car was coasting through like they were looking for an address.

"Just act natural," Assassin told him.

With that said, Assassin and Papoose proceeded down the sidewalk, chopping it up. They went along shooting the shit like they didn't know the cops were there. But they could see them at the corner of their eyes. The police car coasted past them with the officer on the passenger side eyeballing them. The police car suddenly picked up speed and took off. Assassin and Papoose sighed with relief once they were gone.

"That was close. I mean, real close," Papoose told Assassin then glanced over his shoulder. The police car was far up the block now.

"I'm tired of going back and forth with these niggaz, Blood," Assassin said angrily, slamming his fist into his palm for emphasis.

"Yeah, me too," Papoose conceded as he texted on his cellular. He was hitting up someone to pick them up.

"Yo." Assassin tapped his arm to get his attention. "Put the word out, Pap. Let niggaz know I got ten bands for anyone with info on where I can find ya boy, KiMani," he told him. "All I needa know is where his ass at, and I'll have that nigga Montez ghost 'em."

"I got chu."

Chapter Four

KiMani and Arnez made it inside of a neighboring alleyway and pulled off their black sunglasses and red bandanas. Sweat was rolling down their faces and dripping off their chins. They stashed their disguises inside of a black garbage bag loaded with trash. KiMani pulled off his hoodie and gloves and stuffed them inside of the garbage bag as well.

"Uhhhh!"

KiMani looked over his shoulder and saw Arnez wincing as he tried to pull the burnt sleeve of his hoodie off his arm. He'd been burned so badly that the fabric had clung to his flesh like a second skin and had become hard to peel off, like a scab.

"Aaaah, fuck, Blood, this shit hurt! This shit hurts like a mothafucka, on gang!" Arnez swore as he looked at his arm and continued to try to pull it off.

"Keep it on 'til we get to the crib, your DNA gone be clung to it anyway. We dropped a body so the pigs will be able to connect us to it," KiMani said and then paused like a recollection had hit him in the gut like a balled fist. "Matter of fact..." He grabbed the black garbage bag they'd stuffed their disguises inside of and dumped its contents out onto the trashy alley ground. He nudged Arnez and they ran toward the end of the alley. They stopped when they reached the end and looked around for someplace else to run.

"Fuck all this running and shit, we needa whip, Blood," Arnez informed KiMani as he stepped to the driver's window of a money-green Acura. He scanned the area to make sure there weren't any eyes on him before he cocked back his elbow to crack the driver's window. Just as he was about to go through with what he had in mind, the sound of a horn stole his and KiMani's attention. They looked in the direction the honking had come from and found a familiar face in the driver's window of a smoke-gray 1968 Cadillac Eldorado. The sunlight reflected off the classic model vehicle, causing it to gleam in certain areas.

"Come on, nephew!" Lil' Saint hollered out of the window and motioned them over to his Caddy. KiMani and Arnez ran around to the opposite side of the Eldorado, hopping into the backseat. As soon as KiMani slammed the door shut behind them, Lil' Saint drove off, listening to gospel music. The music was softly playing. KiMani and Arnez glanced out the back window and saw a police car driving out of the alley. They sank down into the seat and sighed with relief, wiping the sweat from their foreheads.

Lil' Saint adjusted his round lens, gold-frame glasses and peered into the rearview mirror, which had a gold rosary hanging from it. He watched as the police car that had come out of the alley drove in the opposite direction. A second one came out and came in their direction.

"Unc, they're on us," KiMani announced after stealing another glance through the back window.

"Besides that one following us, there's also one coming up ahead," Lil' Saint informed him as he placed his hand upon the black leather Bible lying on the passenger seat. He gently caressed the gold Holy Cross emblazoned at the center of it. It was his way of summoning up the protection of Almighty God.

"Fuck, man—" Arnez said as he cradled his arm. He was swiftly cut off by Lil' Saint's stern voice.

"Young man, mind your tongue," a frowning Lil' Saint warned him about his foul mouth.

"My bad, OG, I don't mean no disrespect." Arnez winced. His singed arm was aching like hell, and he was dying to get some relief for it.

"If that's your way of apologizing, then I'll accept it for what it's worth," Lil' Saint replied without taking his eyes off the road ahead.

Although the boys were nervous with the police being present, the retired gangsta was cool, calm, and collected. He'd had many run-ins with the law in his day, so the boys in blue didn't make him feel uneasy at all. He'd grown used to them. As a matter of fact, he was familiar with all the badges back in his old neighborhood. They knew each other by names, faces, and reputations. They were aware of Lil' Saint and his father's penchant for murder and their tendency to get away with it. They were known to bring it to anyone—cops, judges, and whomever else, which was why they stayed out of their way, if they could.

The boys sighed with relief when the police cars passed them up. Lil' Saint smiled and patted the Holy Bible on the passenger seat affectionately. Once again, the Lord had shone his light on him in a situation he didn't see himself coming out of.

"Thanks, Unc," a smiling KiMani said, leaning forward and patting Lil' Saint on his shoulder.

"Yeah, good looking out, OG," Arnez chimed in, tapping his fist to his chest.

"Don't thank me, young men, thank the Man upstairs." Lil' Saint held up the Bible. KiMani kissed it and thanked God, then Arnez kissed it and thanked him as well. "Hahahahahahahaha!" Lil' Saint laughed, seeing how silly the boys were.

Suddenly, the car became silent and everyone engrossed with thinking. They all wore serious expressions as they coasted along through the streets.

"In Jesus' name, thank you, Lord," KiMani whispered loud enough for only him to hear. He pulled the gold rosary from out of his shirt and kissed it. He hadn't been religious up until about four years ago. Lil' Saint had turned him on to the word and he'd begun studying it like he was paid to. He attended church every Tuesday, Thursday, and Sunday. He hadn't missed a day since he'd gotten baptized. Still, that didn't stop him from running the streets with Arnez, raising the crime rate and earning a buck. The way he saw it, if he sat on his ass, then God wasn't going to help him, because the good Lord helped those that helped themselves.

Arnez looked at KiMani curiously. He knew he was into the gospel and had seen him pray millions of time. Hell, he even attended church with him a couple of times.

He knew that he and KiMani were lucky to have had their asses pulled out of the fire, and he felt like that was something he should be thanking the Most High for. Mindful of this, Arnez took hold of KiMani's rosary, kissed it, and thanked God Almighty like he had.

KiMani looked at Arnez like something had gotten into him. He was staring out of the back passenger window, but he could feel his best friend's eyes on him. He looked at him, furrowing his forehead.

"What's up?" Arnez shrugged, wondering why the fuck he was staring at him.

"Nothing. Nothing at all," KiMani replied, turning his attention out of the window.

Lil' Saint pulled up in the driveway of KiMani's crib, shifted the gear into park, and allowed his whip to idle. He unbuckled his safety belt and turned around in his seat.

"Who car is this in the driveway?" Lil' Saint asked KiMani.

KiMani looked over his shoulder to get a better look at the whip ahead of them. "Oh, that's my mom's car. I forgot she and Billion were dropping by. We're supposed to eat dinner tonight."

Lil' Saint took a gander at his timepiece and then looked at KiMani. "I would hop out to holla at her for a sec, but I have a few corners I have to bend. So, be sure to say hello to her for me and give her my love."

"Fa sho, Unc, I got chu faded," KiMani assured him.

"Alright then, nephew, I'll rap witchu later," Lil' Saint told him. "I love you, man. See you at church Thursday."

"I love you too, Unc. I'll see you then." KiMani dapped him up and tapped his fist to his chest. Arnez exchanged goodbyes with Lil' Saint, dapped him up, and tapped his fist to his chest too.

KiMani and Arnez hopped out of the old school Cadillac and made their way toward the house. At this time, Lil' Saint backed his way out of the driveway and drove off. Unbeknownst to the boys, a man that was very familiar with them was driving past slowly. He watched as KiMani rapped on the door with Arnez standing behind him. The man had it in his mind to hop out and lay him down. He took his gun from underneath the driver's seat, laid it in his lap, and glanced at his watch. He was sure he wouldn't have enough time to splash KiMani and get to where he needed to be in time.

"Fuck!" The man pounded his fist angrily against the steering wheel. He hated loose ends, but reasoned he could always double back to handle his business. He stared at the address of the home the boys were standing at, reciting it to himself over and over again. Once he was sure he had it memorized, he tucked his blower underneath the driver seat and sped off in a hurry. The loud skirting stole the attention of KiMani and Arnez, who were still standing at the door of his house. When they looked up, they could see the car that had been spying on them speeding away.

"Yo, you know who that was?" KiMani asked Arnez. His forehead was creased with wonder.

A frowning Arnez was still staring at the speeding car over his shoulder when he answered, "I'm not sure, but we gotta stay on point from now on. Ain't no telling if that was the opps or not."

I think that was Unc's ride, but I'm not 'bouta mention that shit to Ki. He'll definitely feel like he's a threat with knowledge of him knowing where he lays his head. If the homie ever became wise to that, then he'd prowl the streets looking for Unc to blow 'em away, Arnez thought. *I'ma just keep this bit of info to myself, and just holla at Unc once time permits it.*

"Blood, what the fuck are you thinking about? Bring yo' ass on," KiMani told Arnez as Lachaun held open the front door.

"Oh, my bad," Arnez said, snapping back out of his thoughts and heading inside of the house behind KiMani.

"Hey, what's up, Arnez?" Lachaun greeted him with the biggest smile.

"What up, Chaun?" Arnez replied, wincing from his aching arm.

Lachaun playfully smacked the back of his head and said, "Boy, what I tell you about that?"

"My bad, *ma.*" Arnez grinned.

"Jesus Christ." She frowned up, seeing his burnt arm. "What the hell happened to your arm?" she asked as she locked the door behind him and closed the other one.

KiMani gave her the rundown of the drama between them and Hitt-Man's people while he rifled through the refrigerator. He then told her about the situation that led to Arnez's arm being fried, leaving out the part where he'd bodied Lil' D.

KiMani pulled out a small bottle of Motts apple juice from the fridge, screwed off the cap, and took a drink. He then rummaged through the cabinets for a bottle of Jack Daniels. Once he found it, he took it down and headed back toward the living room.

"I never thought he'd take over Caleb's organization. I always thought of him as more of the muscle," Lachaun said. "Everybody wants to be the man, I guess." She took Arnez by his hand and led him over to the living room table. She directed him to sit down, and she sat down in front of him. Her forehead was wrinkled as she examined his badly burned arm closely. "Billllion!" she called out to her son.

"Yes, Mommy!" Billion called out from KiMani's bedroom where he was playing his PS4.

"Get me the yellow first-aid kit out from under the bathroom sink, please!" Lachaun told him as she continued to examine Arnez's arm. He watched her as he took the occasional swallow of Jack Daniel's. He made ugly faces as the dark liquor seared his belly.

"Okay," Billion replied.

Everyone inside of the living room could hear Billion running back and forth inside of the house. This included KiMani, who was posted up behind Arnez rolling up a blunt fat enough to make a Rastafarian proud. The idea was to get Arnez as shit-faced as he possibly could, so he wouldn't have to deal with the pain of Lachaun taking care of his arm.

"Here you go, Mommy." Billion walked the yellow first-aid kit over to his mother. He was happy to see his other brother and his best friend present. He looked up to them. They were legends in his eyes and couldn't do any wrong.

"Thank you, baby." Lachaun kissed him and caressed the side of his face.

"What up, baby boy?" Arnez greeted him and dapped him up.

"What's up, Arnez? Dang, what happened to yo' arm?" Billion's brows furrowed, looking at the young man's fried arm. His shit looked like a slab of ribs fresh off the grill. "I hadda, uh, an, uh…" He looked at Lachaun for a lie he could give the kid.

"Car accident, baby. Arnez hadda car accident." Lachaun informed him.

"Wow. A car accident got his arm looking like that?" Billion asked.

"Yep. A very bad one, too," Lachaun said.

"Sure was," KiMani chimed in, holding a blunt in one hand and sprinkling weed inside of it with the other. "Arnez was trying to show off to a couple of girls and messed around and slammed into a tree. The front of his whip exploded on impact and went up in flames. Yo' big bro hadda save 'em too. 'Cause had I not, he'd be wearing a halo and white gown now."

"My hero," Arnez said in a feminine voice, smiling. "Yo, Ki, hurry up with that bleezy. I'm tryna put something in the air. You know liquor ain't never really been my thang."

"Man, Arnez, you should be a superhero," Billion said as he walked around Arnez, studying him closely. "You've been shot, stabbed, and now you've been set on fire. Man, you're invincible, can't nothing kill you. You've got more lives than a cat."

Lachaun, Arnez, and KiMani busted up laughing.

"This lil' nigga funny as a mothafucka," KiMani declared with a smile. He'd just placed the blunt in his mouth and fired up the tip of it. He sucked on the end of it and blew out a big cloud of smoke. He then hung his arm around Billion's shoulders and continued to indulge in the potent Kush. "You've been practicing boxing like I showed you, huh?" KiMani looked down at his little brother with a grin on his lips. He let smoke billow from his nostrils and mouth.

"Unh, huh," Billion said with a smile.

"Oh, yeah? Well, we're about to see." KiMani passed the smoldering blunt to Arnez. He then took his arm from around his little brother and got into a fighting stance. He threw up his fists. "Come on, baby boy, throw yo' shit up."

"KiMani!" Lachaun said as she picked out the fabric embedded in Arnez's burned arm. She didn't like anyone cussing around Billion. She'd been a fairly strict parent when it came to him, and rightfully so. She didn't want him coming up like her, his father, and his older brother had.

"My bad, Ma, I didn't mean to say that shi—" his eyes widened as he caught himself before he could say the full word. Lachaun frowned and twisted her lips. She sat the tweezers down on the table top she'd been using to pick the pieces of fabric from Arnez's arm and turned around to KiMani. He looked worried as hell. He knew of his mother's reputation in the streets, and he didn't want any smoke with her. "Stuff, Ma. That's what I meant to say, stuff."

"Alright now, boy, you gon' make me snatch them lips right off yo' face. Keep on," Lachaun said, and picked the tweezers back up to complete the task at hand.

"Come on now, lil' bro, put cho fists up like I taught chu," KiMani told Billion. He was still facing him with his fists up and his feet position in a fighter's stance. Billion got into a fighting stance like his big brother. "Show me what chu got, lil' man."

KiMani threw opened hands at Billion to not hurt him, but the boy bobbed and weaved his attack like a professional fighter. He then countered back with a combination of punches of his own. He was moving precise and fast. The year he'd spent under his older brother's tutelage had done him good. There weren't too many kids his age that could see him with hands and footwork.

"Alright, that's what I'm talking about." KiMani smiled and gave Billion an exclusive handshake that he shared between him and Arnez. He hung his arm around his little brother's shoulders and took the bleezy Arnez was extending in his direction. "So, Madukes, what's on the menu for the night?"

"Oxtails, yams, Chinese mustard greens, mac and cheese, and corn bread," Lachaun replied as she helped Arnez out of his hoodie so she could apply some ointment to his arm.

"Now that sounds good," Arnez said to no one in particular.

"I love oxtails," Billion said.

"Me too, baby boy," KiMani claimed. "I'ma tear that down. Thanks for coming over to cook for me, Momma." He hugged her around her neck, pressing his cheek against her, and then kissed her on the cheek.

"You're welcome, son," Lachaun told him. "Arnez, you're family too. You're welcome to stay for dinner."

"Oh, I was gon' show up if you didn't invite me anyway," Arnez admitted with a grin. "All that food you're talking about whipping up sounds too good for me to miss out on."

Everyone laughed.

"So, Ma, exactly what day are they gon' let Pops out this week?" KiMani inquired with a serious look on his face.

"I'm not sure yet," Lachaun said, applying the ointment to a wincing Arnez's arm. "He said he'd let me know before the week's out, though. Have you talked to 'em?"

"He hit me up a few times, but I've been onna move so I haven't had time to holla at 'em yet," KiMani told her. "I shot 'em a text though."

"Oh yeah? What chu tell 'em?" she asked as she placed gauze up Arnez's arm. "Billion, baby, gemme that Ace bandage outta the first-aid kit, would you? Please." She extended her hand and waited for her son to hand her what she'd asked for. Billion gave her what she requested and stood beside her. He watched carefully as his mother wrapped the beige bandage snuggly around Arnez's arm. The entire time, the young man watched her while taking pulls from the blunt KiMani had given back to him.

"Same ol', same ol', you know, the usual," KiMani replied. "I love 'em. I miss 'em. I can't wait for 'em to come home."

"That's good," Lachaun said, still wrapping up Arnez's arm. "Are you excited for your dad to come home, Billion?"

"Yes." Billion smiled, jumping up and down. "I can't wait 'til he comes home. We'll finally get to be a real family then." He grabbed his mother by the face and kissed her on her lips. She blushed and smiled. She absolutely loved when her children showed her affection. It was one of the best parts about being a mother.

"Oh, yeah, Ma," KiMani called for his mother's attention. He'd just recalled something. "Uncle Saint dropped us off. He said to tell you what's up? And to give you his love."

"Lil' Saint, huh? That's my nigga," Lachaun said. "How come he didn't come inside? I haven't seen 'em inna while."

"He was but he said he hadda few corners he hadda bend," KiMani reported.

"Yeah, that sounds like ol' Saint...always on the go," Lachaun said. "Okay, Mr. Arnez, I've finished wrapping your arm."

Arnez looked at his arm admiringly. He was pleased with the job she'd done. "Thanks, Chaun."

"Boy, how many times do I have to tell you to call me ma or momma?" Lachaun said with a playful attitude. "You're a part of this family too. As far as I'm concerned, I have three handsome young men."

Arnez smiled and nodded. He loved the fact that Lachaun always treated him like she'd pushed him out of her womb. He loved being a part of the James family. "Thanks, Ma."

"Now that's more like it. Eventually, you'll get used to it." Lachaun smirked, rubbing the top of his head and then kissing him on the cheek. She then started placing all of the items back inside of the yellow first-aid kit. Next, she closed it, handed it to Billion, and told him to put it back where he'd gotten it. "Hurry up, baby boy, I'm tryna make a quick run to the store."

"But we already went to the store, Ma." Billion frowned in confusion.

"I know, baby, but I forgot a couple of things I needa cook with. Now, chop, chop!" Lachaun hurried him along, clapping her hands rapidly. She smacked him on his butt and he ran off to the bathroom.

Lachaun picked up her purse and swung its strap around her shoulder. She took a stick of gum out of it, popped it in her mouth, and started chewing it. By this time, Billion had returned from putting up the first-aid kit in the bathroom. "Ready to go, baby boy?"

54

"Yep," Billion replied jovially.

"Good. Tell yo' brothers goodbye," Lachaun said.

Billion dapped up KiMani and Arnez. Lachaun blew the boys a kiss before she and Billion left the house.

"Aye, nigga, you know this shit don't stop, right?" KiMani asked as he returned to the living room. He'd just shut and locked the door behind his mother and brother.

Arnez raised an eyebrow as he was taking a drink from the bottle of Jack. He wiped his wet mouth with the hand he clutched the bottle in. "What chu getting at, kid?"

KiMani pulled out his cellphone and a chair, and straddled it backwards. "Blood, we gon' keep coming at these fuck niggaz' necks 'til they lying in the streets bleeding," he vowed. "What we need are some bulletproof vests."

"Yeah, but where the fuck are we gonna get 'em?" Arnez asked.

"Kramer's ol' crooked-ass," KiMani replied as he searched his contacts. "Nigga One Time. They're known for confiscating niggaz' shit and not reporting it."

Arnez smiled and slapped hands with him. "Now, you're talking, big dog, hit that fool up."

"Fa sho'," KiMani replied and pressed the call button on his cellular. Detective Kramer picked up after three rings. "What up? Yeah, it's me. Listen, I needa get my hands onna couple bullet-proof vests."

Chapter Five
Three nights later

"Alright, playas, ballas, scammers, dope boys and kingpins, I'ma need you to break bread and show some love for one of our favorites—Xena, Thee Body!" DJ Flip, a five-foot-six, dark-complexioned nigga sporting short locs, introduced one of the most popular performers of the night. A second later, the lights went out in the club, and a spotlight shone on the stage's curtains. The curtains parted and a six-foot mahogany goddess sashayed out. Her hourglass shape was thick and luscious. Her breasts were the size of melons, and her ass was so big you could saddle it like a horse for a ride.

Drake's "Shut it Down" filled the air as Xena Thee Body walked down the stage like a superstar runway model. She had a katana in either hand and they were both dried in a flammable substance. She was wearing yellow cat-eye contacts. The black mask that covered the lower half of her face made her look like a ninja. Her white knotless, fourteen-inch individual braids bounced with each step she took. She was wearing a floor-length, see-through robe. Her waist was enclosed in a black leather waistband. The areolas of her breasts were visible through the robe, but the black leather thong hid her bald pussy well.

Boom! Boom! Boom! Boom!
Frooosh! Frooosh! Frooosh! Frooosh!

Fireballs erupted from the corners of the stage, startling men sitting at tables nearby. The roaring fires settled down and licked the air consistently. Xena Thee Body stopped at the center of the stage and started dancing seductively as Drake continued to croon.

But I just always feel like they're in need of something you got
It's obvious you're pretty
Heard that you're a student working weekends in the city
Tryna take you out girl, hope you're not too busy

As Xena Thee Body danced seductively, using the katanas, she sliced off her mask and strips of her robe. When she was done, she was wearing her black leather thong. Right then, thirsty ass niggaz hooted, hollered, clapped their hands, and threw dead presidents up at her. The money went up into the air and came down like confetti, coating the stage. While she continued her dancing, Xena Thee Body's alluring eyes came across Papoose's and held onto him. It was like she had cast a spell upon him, all he could do was stand there firing crisp one-dollar bills at her.

Xena Thee Body stuck out her abnormally long pierced tongue and coiled it at Papoose. It was as if her tongue was calling him over to her. She flipped the hilts of her twin katanas over in her hands, formed an "X" below her waist, and then swept them across each other.

Sniiiiikt!

Frooosh!

Sparks flew as the katanas came across each other and a burst of flames traveled up their full-length. Still keeping her eyes on Papoose, Xena Thee Body tilted her head back and slowly slid the burning blade down her throat. She stopped at the hilt extinguishing the flame, impressing all of the men watching her and continuously throwing their hard-earned money. She stabbed the katana into the stage and took the other flaming sword into her mouth, down to the hilt. Once she extinguished the flame, she stabbed the katana into the stage. Next, she placed her palms on the bottoms of the hilts and stood upside down on them. She opened her thick legs and spread them in all directions. She came back down to the stage one leg at a time. Next, she jumped on top of the bottoms of the katanas and kept dancing seductively. She kept her eyes on Papoose as she yanked the black leather thong from her body and threw them at Papoose. It landed on the youngsta's face. He snatched it off, inhaled its scent, and smiled like he'd been accepted into heaven.

Papoose tucked the thong into his back pocket as the men looked at him with jealousy. He kept his eyes on her and she kept her eyes on him. He loaded the money gun with a stack of fresh, crisp one-dollar bills and pointed it at her. He pulled the trigger of it and money flowed out of it rapidly. Xena Thee Body danced in the money he shot at her, treating the falling currency like droplets of rain.

"That's my new favorite bitch up there, Blood!" Papoose told Assassin without taking his eyes off Xena Thee Body. He was enchanted by her presence and hypnotic dancing. "I'm telling you, dog, I don't give a fuck! If I could I'd get that ho pregnant, and marry her ass!"

"Yeah, I bet cho ol' thirsty ass would!" Assassin laughed and took the bottle of Ace of Spades to the head, guzzling it. A little of the expensive champagne spilled down his chin and he wiped it away. He then scanned the area looking for a stripper to take up time with. "Where that bitch, Beauty, at Blood? I'm tryna fuck something." When his eyes landed on a light-skinned, slim-thick chick in a lime green bikini, he called out to her. She was in the middle of giving some young, white college kid a lap dance. The cherry blonde-haired, blue-eyed youth had a red lipstick imprint kiss on his cheek and two hands full of dollar bills secured by rubber bands. A few other girls were giving his buddies a lap dance. They all were either smoking fat ass cigars and/or sipping dark liquor. They all seemed to be solely focused on all of the jiggling ass and titties in front of them.

"Bro, you're not gonna get that bitch's attention that way," Papoose assured him. "Money talks with these hoes. I thought chu knew." He passed Assassin one of his money guns while he held on to the other. He tapped him on his shoulder and said something into his ear, and he nodded his understanding. Together, they pointed their money guns at Beauty and shot a line of dead white men in her direction. The bills deflected off of the scantily dressed dancer. She looked up at Assassin and smiled, holding up one finger for him to give her a minute, she was almost finished performing for the college kid.

"Blood, this bitch needa hurry up, I'm tryna slide up in some-thing," Assassin announced. His eyes were glued on Beauty as he adjusted his hard piece in his jeans. "Come down, Damage," he addressed his dick. "I know you're hungry, I'ma feed you. Relax."

Right then, the music switched to a throwback song that was known to get the parties jumping in the early two-thousands: Jay-Z's "I Just Wanna Love U."

Hov', unstoppable, Dynasty, young Hova
I'm a hustler baby (I'm a hustler)
I just want you to know (Wanna let you know)
It ain't where I been (It ain't where I been)

Right then, Xena Thee Body squatted down and started popping her pussy and twerking. Two niggaz with handfuls of dead white men climbed up on stage. One was an older, balding white man in a short-sleeve plaid shirt, and the other was a brother wearing icy platinum jewelry over a Givenchy crewneck sweatshirt. Xena ground into the lap of the white dude while she held the waist of the brother. The brother's tongue hung out of his mouth, and he was dropping twenty-dollar bills on her one at a time.

Xena looked over her shoulder and found Papoose still watching her. He sat his money gun down upon the tabletop and pulled out a big ass brick of blue face hundred-dollar bills. He held the colorful bills up and motioned Xena Thee Body over. She shoved the white man and the brother aside and signaled for her handlers to bag up the money she'd earned during her performance. Next, she walked to the edge of the stage where one of her handlers, who was holding onto a bag, helped her down. Xena Thee Body sauntered towards Papoose with that big old ass of hers swinging from left to right. She grabbed him by the front of his shirt and pulled him along. He followed her lead with a big ass smile across his face.

Assassin turned around in his chair, smiling and watching his homeboy being carried away. Papoose looked over his shoulder at his dog and mouthed, "I'm 'bouta fuck the shit outta this bitch." Assassin doubled over laughing with his hand on his stomach. He sat back up and saluted him. Shortly thereafter, Beauty walked over after finishing her lap dance with the white dude. She took Assassin by his hand and led him towards the back of the club.

This was where patrons went to get sucked and fucked for a fee. There's no business like ho business!

Unbeknownst to Assassin and Papoose, JayDee and Hot Boy were sitting in the back of the club, hidden within the shadows, watching them closely. They'd noticed how freely Assassin and Papoose had been spending money. They hadn't just tricked off at the gentlemen's club, but they'd torn down the malls and swap meets as well. On top of that, they'd gone car and motorcycle shopping. Assassin had copped a midnight-blue Mercedes Benz S-Class and an ox-blood-red Ducati Monster. Papoose, on the other hand, settled on a milk-white Porsche 911 Carrera coupe and a bumblebee-yellow Yamaha 600 class sports bike. They were even going to see about buying a boat, but by the time they'd arrived on the lot, the place was already closed.

Now, Assassin and Papoose weren't broke-ass niggaz by any stretch of the imagination. But they definitely didn't have the bags to drop on the items they'd picked up. This wasn't a good look for them since their boss had gotten robbed for a shipment.

JayDee and Hot Boy declined a couple of lap dances and tossed back what was left of their drinks. JayDee placed a ten-dollar tip on the tabletop and sat his empty glass on it. There wasn't any doubt in his mind the young niggaz highjacked Hitt-Man's heroin shipment, and he was going to give him his report now. Walking across the club, he pulled out his cellphone and hit up his boss to inform him of his findings. Hitt-Man picked up as JayDee looked over his shoulder at Assassin and Papoose. The two of them disappeared into a different rooms on opposite sides of the hallway.

"Yeah, man, they're up here now spending mad dough..." JayDee told Hitt-Man.

***

After Zekey took a leak, he wandered over to the bathroom sink. He turned on the faucet water and soaped up his hands while eying his reflection in the medicine cabinet mirror. His hair was beginning to grow back, so his receding hairline was visible and so was his salt and pepper goatee. Zekey was thankful for the privilege of being able to grow old. He'd barely made it home from the five-year stretch he'd completed a year ago for armed robbery. His beef with Changa, Travieso's uncle, spilled inside of prison and several attempts were made on his life. If it hadn't been for the brothers holding him down, he was sure he would have been a goner.

Although it was hell behind those barbwire fences with a bounty on his head and a monkey on his back, the time he spent incarcerated wasn't all bad. He managed to kick his habit and found the love of his life—Quan. They'd met each other while he was locked up. She was the homegirl of his celly's girlfriend. She wasn't expecting anything to come out of her conversing with him, but an unexpected romance occurred. They caught feelings for each other rather quickly, but neither of them could deny the chemistry between them.

Zekey stopped rinsing his hands and looked at the wedding ring. The thought of his lovely wife, who was getting ready for bed then, brought a smirk to his lips. He turned off the faucet and started drying his hands on a towel on the rack. Hearing knocking at the door, he stopped drying his hands and looked at it.

"Hold on. I'm finna—" Zekey began, but before he could finish, the bathroom door was opening. He turned around and Quan entered, shutting and locking the door behind her. When she turned back around to Zekey, he was smiling and rubbing his hands together. He was dying to be in between her legs. He loved fucking his wife, not only was she desirable, but the sex got better each time they got down. She may have been a lady in the streets but between the sheets, she was a straight-up nymphomaniac. Sure, she was shy the first few times they'd gotten busy, but once she'd gotten comfortable she showed up and showed out. She'd done shit in bed with him he'd never experienced with any other woman. And he couldn't get enough of it!

"Damn, lil' mama, you looking good as fuck," Zekey told her, taking in her appearance from head to toe. Quan stood five-foot-five and had a coffee-brown complexion. She kept her knotless braids rolled up on either side of her hair like Princess Leia. She had the pretty light-brown eyes and big pillow-soft lips. A diamond stud nose ring was in her right nostril. Her breasts were huge and her ass was even bigger. She was wearing a black see-through teddy that didn't leave shit to imagination. Her dark skin tone set off her white French-tip-manicured fingernails and toenails. Little mama was two hundred and thirty pounds of sexiness, and Zekey felt like the luckiest man in the world. And why wouldn't he? He was about five minutes away from fucking her.

"Oh, really?" Quan smiled and blushed. She loved the way he looked at her. It was like he couldn't believe she belonged to him, and that made her feel beautiful. It also made her want to fulfill his every need in and out of the bedroom.

"Hell yeah, youz bad as fuck, ma." Zekey stepped before her and placed his hands on her hips. "You gotta nigga wanting you bad as hell, straight drop, no cuts," he swore. "Man, you smelling hella good, too." He closed his eyes and inhaled the enchanted fragrance on her neck.

Zekey placed gentle kisses on Quan's shoulder up to her neck. He nibbled and sucked on her earlobe then whispered all of the nasty things he wanted to do to her while groping her titties. His hot breath and sexual voice against her ear made her moist between her meaty thighs, and her clit stiffened. She closed her eyes and tilted her head back as Zekey licked along her jawline and then sucked on the soft flesh just below her chin. Instantly, her big nipples became engorged and poked out like a baby's toes.

"Ssssssss, aaaahhhh," Quan whined as Zekey continued to suck on her neck while popping her titties out of her teddy. He licked down her neck and gently bit down it as he pulled on her nipples. She rubbed the back of his head and moaned. She could feel the wetness of her vagina running down either side of her legs. Zekey grabbed two handfuls of her breasts encircling her areolas with his tongue and then sucking on their nipples. He groaned as he sucked thirstily from her bosom. The sounds of him feasting on her tits were driving her insane. Her eyes fluttered and her mouth hung open. "Uh, uh, uh, uh, oh, daddy, that—that—that feels—feels so—so good." She stammered, feeling more of her natural juices sliding down between her thighs.

Zekey released one of Quan's bosoms and focused on one. He stuck his thumb inside of Quan's mouth and she sucked on it. He trailed his other hand down her protruding stomach, which was covered in stretch marks from bearing her first and only child. He pulled her black thong aside and her fat pussy lips popped out. She placed her pretty foot on the tub to grant him full access to her pink valley. He rubbed on her dripping kitty and it slicked his fingers wet. He stuck two of his fingers inside of her and pressed his thumb against her clit. He finger fucked her rapidly while stimulating her clit with his thumb. He did this while kissing all over her face, sucking on her lips and tongue.

"Oh, oh, daddy, I'm 'bouta—I'm 'bouta have an—have an orgasm!" Quan's eyes rolled to the back of her head and her mouth trembled. Zekey scowled and gripped her ass up by her neck. She gasped loudly. That shit turned her on! "Ahhhh, ahhhh, ahhhh! Here I—here I cummmmmmmm!" She went crazy, shaking uncontrollably as a clear fluid sprayed from between her legs. It splashed all over Zekey's arm, legs, and bare feet. "I can't take it—I can't take it, daddy," she said, looking him in his eyes.

"Shut up! Shut cho ass up and gemme my shit," Zekey said through clenched teeth, squeezing her neck tighter.

"Spit on me, spit on me, baby!" Quan shouted louder and louder.

"Oh, you want me to spit on you, you nasty ass bitch? Okay." Zekey harped up and spat on her face. She told him to do it again and he spat on her two more times. A string of saliva hung from his bottom lip to his chin. It glistened in the light of the bathroom.

"Oh, fuck, yes, yes!" Her eyes showed whiteness as she threw her head back. Veins bulged on her forehead and neck. Another orgasm was building up between her legs and she was about to explode again. "Keep spitting on me, daddy! Keep spitting on me!" she shouted at him.

Zekey spat on her repeatedly while continuing to finger fuck her faster and faster. Before he knew it, she was screaming at the top of her lungs and more of the fluid sprayed out of her. Her pussy was like a small fire hose drenching everything in front of her. She felt like all of the energy had been zapped out of her, and she collapsed to the floor. She lay there with her hands between her legs and squeezing her thighs together. She closed her eyes and moaned sensually. Her clit was sensitive and her essence was flowing freely from her vagina.

Zekey pulled off his wife beater and threw it aside. He then pulled down his boxer briefs and pajama pants and kicked them aside. He stood over Quan, smiling and stroking his long fat dick up and down. A clear fluid seeped out of its pee-hole and dripped from his mushroom tip.

"Get cho thick ass up, I want some of my pussy," Zekey told her, leaning down and smacking her on her big old ass. He stood upright and watched her pull off her teddy and then her thong. She got up from the floor and stood upright in all of her glory. Although she was a big girl, she had an hourglass shape. Still holding his piece in his hand, Zekey took her in from head to toe once more. He made note of her piercings. Though he'd seen them before, for some reason, they stood out now. The studs in both her nipples and clit gleamed. And so did the diamonds in her engagement ring and her platinum wedding ring.

Zekey approached Quan and grabbed her by the throat roughly. He walked her back until she bumped up against the door. He licked her lips, sucked on them, and kissed her diligently. They made out with their eyes closed, turning their heads in opposite directions. The sound of their saliva and smacking lips filled the bathroom. Their passionate session made them both aroused. They were dying to get it in. Zekey groped and rubbed all over Quan's buttocks. She threw her arms around his neck as they continued tonguing each other down.

"Whoooo!" Quan's eyes exploded open as she hollered out. Zekey had abruptly hoisted her legs around his waist and carried her over to the bathtub. He told her to grab hold of the rod that held up the shower curtain. She did just that and they kissed some more. "Daddy, you—you can hold me up?" she asked as he gently bit into the side of her neck and sucked on it.

"Don't worry about nothing, mamas, yo' man got chu," Zekey assured her and hoisted her further up on him. He then spread his legs apart and grabbed hold of his piece. He slid the head of his shit up and down her slit, coating it with her juice. Next, he tapped his meat against her clit and rubbed it back and forth across it. He looked back and forth between her pleasured face and what he was doing. His face was a mask of concentration, and his eyes projected his determination to make her orgasm again.

"Ooooooh, daddy, here I cum again! Oooooh, shiiiiiit!" Quan said, throwing her head back and then launching it forward. Her eyes exploded open again, and her mouth hung open. Her arms and legs shook wildly. A second later, she was spraying Zekey again and dripping on the floor. That shit turned him on. He was ready to slide up in her now. And with the way that big old pussy of hers was gushing, he was sure he wouldn't have any problem pushing past her threshold.

Zekey placed Quan's legs on either side of his head as she held on to the rod. Her eyes were hooded, and she was breathing heavily. That last orgasm had taken a lot out of her, but she was definitely up for more. Zekey held onto her right leg as he took hold of himself and placed his dick at her slick entrance.

"Aaaaah, fuck," Zekey said under his breath as he slowly slid himself inside of Quan. Her shit was slippery wet and as hot as an oven. Her walls accommodated girth and width of Zekey's piece. He tilted his head downward and bit down on his bottom lip. He slipped his strong, masculine hands around Quan's thighs and took hold of them from the inside. He began to thrust in and out of her faster and faster, drawing a moan from his lips. The faster he went, the louder she became, and his nut sack rocked back and forth. Veins etched up and down Quan's forehead and neck as she squeezed her eyes shut. She basked in the blissful moment as he gave it to her fast, hard, and steady. "Nuh unh, you look at me, bitch! You look at me while I'm fucking you!" he demanded, with

66

anger in his tone, and started pounding her out. Her eyes exploded open again, and she maintained eye contact with him. He gripped her thighs tighter and humped into her with a vengeance. Beads and beads of sweat oozed out of the pores of his face and body. A droplet of sweat fell from the corner of his brow while the rest slid down his form.

Bop, bop, bop, bop, bop, bop!

Zekey's perspiring body sounded like a shotgun firing repeatedly as it smacked into Quan's. Sweat fell from the both of them like raindrops and splashed on the floor. Their heavy breathing and skin smacking resonated throughout the bathroom.

Bop, bop, bop, bop, bop, bop!

The smacking and heavy breathing grew louder. The louder they got, the faster the sweat fell, and more of it collected on the floor below.

"Ah, ah, ah, aaah! Spit on me, daddy! Spit on me!" Quan begged and hollered. Zekey's sweat leaped from his body each time his hot, sticky body collided with her. He harped and spat on her repeatedly, and consistently threw dick up in her. He was hitting her spot. The sex felt amazing to them both. Her tight WAP created friction around his dick head and stimulated him to great heights. "Oh, yes, yes, fuck me! Fuck me!"

"Grrrrr!" Zekey's face balled up and he bowed his head. He held her thighs even tighter and jack-hammered that pussy.

Bop, bop, bop, bop, bop, bop!

Zekey's pelvis was moving so fast it started to look like a blur. Sweat was flying from both of them and heat was escaping from their bodies. The temperature was rising inside of the bathroom and the mirror began to fog.

Quan, gripping the rod tighter, threw her head back. "Uh, uh, uh, uh, uh! I'm cuming, I'm cuming, I'm cuming, daddy. Don't stop! Please, don't stop!"

Zekey grinded his teeth and growled like a wild animal. The nigga was sweating so much it looked like he'd swam a lap in the pool before hopping out.

"Here I cuuummmm!" Quan screamed loud enough to wake the neighbors, and then she came hard as a mothafucka, every foot of her shook like she was being shocked in an electric chair.

Once Quan regain her composure, she threw her arms around Zekey's neck and he took her away from the shower rod. They made out as he sat her down on the side of the bathtub. He placed his foot on the tub, took hold of his dick, and motioned Quan over. She crawled over to him like a cheetah looking to pounce on its prey. Her titties jiggled and her big ass swayed from left to right with every movement. "Sssssss! Lick my ass and jack my shit—hurry up!" He motioned her over.

"Nah." Quan licked her lips and groped her breasts. "Not until you say, right now, you dirty fucking bitch!"

"Right. Now. You. Dirty. Fucking. Bitch!" Zekey said like she told him. His face was scrunched with intensity. He wanted and needed that nut like it was his next breath. Quan started pumping his dick and licking his hairy asshole. A smile spread across his lips, and he closed his eyes. "Aaah, yes, yes, you nasty, lil' bitch. Yeah, yeah, you know how daddy likes it! You know exactly what you're doing too!"

"Mmmmmummmmm." Quan sucked on his crinkle, flicking it with her warm, wet tongue while pumping his piece feverishly. The sensation was incredible to him. It brought him up to his toes and had him moaning like a little bitch. His mouth hung open and he held his head back. He held one hand behind his back and placed the other one on her shoulder.

"Ah, aah, aaah, aaaah, shiii—shiii—shiiiit!" Zekey said with veins bulging over his face and body. He could feel his balls swelling with his gooey semen and his mushroom tip becoming engorged.

"Mmmmmummmmm." Quan continued manipulating the tight hole below his nutsack and pumping his manhood. Her eyes were closed as she did all this with intensity.

"Yeah, yeah, here I cum! Here I fucking cum, bitch!" Zekey said, taking his dick back and holding Quan back. She tilted her head back, flicked her pierced tongue at him, and rubbed on her clit hard. She held eye contact with him while she did this! He frowned and his nostrils flared. He was squeezing and stroking his dick up and down fast. "Aaaaaaaah!" he roared like a ferocious lion, steadily stroking his shit. Rope after rope of his hot, slimy, white semen shot out of his pee-hole and painted her face. Quan smiled gratefully as she received his gift. Even after his children were hanging from her chin, he was still jacking his shit.

Zekey took a breath and smiled with relief after relieving himself on his wife's face. He lay down on the floor, hot, sweaty, and sticky, with a thudding heart. He closed his eyes and listened to the flowing water as Quan went about washing her face. After drying her face off, she laid her head on his shoulder and traced his muscular chest and abs with her finger.

"Damn, babe, that was—that was—fucking fantastic," Quan said with her eyes closed, smiling.

"Oh, yeah?" Zekey said with his eyes still closed.

"For real, for real." She turned his face to her and kissed him.

Boom, boom, boom, boom!

Rapid pounding on the bathroom door startled Zekey and Quan. They sat up where they were laying and exchanged worried glances.

"Mom, I gotta pee, open up!" Quan's son, Ali, called out from the other side of the door.

Chapter Six
One night later

Zekey stood below the shade of a tree at Trinity Park, occasionally glancing at his watch. He'd gotten word through one of his homeboys that Assassin was offering ten bands for the whereabouts of KiMani. He remembered seeing him outside of a house over on 21st and San Pedro a few days ago. He'd started to bust a bitch and smoke his young ass, but he had other business to attend to, so he decided to let KiMani keep his life for now.

Zekey was still hot from the night KiMani busted him in his mouth and nearly split his wig. If it hadn't been for Arnez knocking the gun away, he would have surely killed him. Although the bullet didn't pierce him, the gun went off dangerously close to his ear and caused him to go deaf. In fact, he'd been wearing a hearing aid since that day. He was self-conscious about having to wear the device on his ear, but he later became comfortable wearing it. Most people had confused the hearing aid with a Bluetooth. Thank God for advanced technology!

After wrapping up his business, Zekey decided to dip back to the house where he'd seen KiMani and Arnez. On his way over, he ran into his homeboy in traffic and they got to chopping it up. That's when he found out about the bread Assassin had put up for information that would lead him to KiMani's whereabouts. His homeboy had a number and everything to get in contact with old boy. Zekey programmed the name and contact into his cell phone, grabbed himself an enchilada plate from Taco Mama, and went home. He ate and fell asleep. But as soon as he got up, he hollered at Assassin and they made plans to link up.

Now, he was going to go through with murdering KiMani himself. But the way he looked at it, he could use those ten stacks Assassin had put up. Sure, his wife had some loot, but that was her dough. He was a grown man and felt comfortable having his *own* bag.

"Where the fuck is this dude? Nigga was 'pose to have been here forty-five minutes ago. I don't have all goddamn night, shit," Zekey bitched and complained, tapping his sneaker impatiently.

Blood, fuck all this waiting and shit. I'ma give this nigga ten more minutes, then I'm out this bitch! I'll slide by youngin's crib and do 'em myself.

Zekey began nodding off and snoring from his consumption of the dope. But the crunching of twigs beneath someone's shoe brought him around. Swiftly, he spun off the back of the tree, pulled his gun, and came back around on the opposite side of it. He dropped down on one knee and aimed his piece in the direction he'd heard the noise coming from.

At the end of his gun, he found a young man standing before him. He was well hidden by the shadows. As a matter of fact, the only thing Zekey could make out of him was his jeans and sneakers. The young man didn't flinch when the blower had been pointed at him. To Zekey's surprise, he seemed calm with a banga in his face. This came from years of being behind the gun and also being at its mercy. He understood there was a thin line between life and death. And every day could quite possibly be his last.

"Are you Assassin?" Zekey asked the man. He couldn't identify the hitta by appearance, but he most definitely knew him by reputation.

"No. Are you Zekey?"

"Yeah. Now, who the fuck are you?"

"You can call me Montez," he answered coolly. "I work for Assassin."

With the understanding of who was standing in front of him, Zekey stood upright and tucked his piece at the small of his back.

"You shoulda said that off top, nigga. I was seconds away from popping yo' ass," Zekey admitted. "You mind doing me a favor and stepping into the light? I'd like to see who I'm talking to."

Montez stepped into what little light the park provided so that Zekey could see his face. He was five-foot-nine and of mixed heritage. His mother was a white woman from Germany, and his father was a black man from Trinidad. He was a Michael Ealy looking-ass nigga with the same golden-brown complexion and blue eyes. The only differences between them were his freckled face, long auburn locs, and his love affair with the streets.

"Better now?"

"Much, nigga."

"Shall we get down to business?"

"I wanna know what the fuck took you so long, bruh? I was 'bouta bounce on yo' ass," Zekey told him with a frown. The fact that Montez had him waiting in the cold for so long had him hot. He was an old school gangsta—an OG. He didn't take disrespect from anyone, especially not from some young ass, wet behind the ears nigga who was in diapers when he was in the streets creating his legacy.

"I've been here—on time, I might add," Montez confessed to Zekey's surprised. Zekey looked at him like, *then what the fuck were you doing this entire time?* "I clung to the shadows, watching you. I had to make sure you weren't trying to set me up."

"Now why in the fuck would I be setting you up?"

"How was Assassin 'pose to know you weren't working for the opps?" Montez asked seriously. "For all he knew, KiMani coulda gotten wind of the money he put up for his location, and set this trap to have his head knocked off."

Zekey nodded understandingly. "Well, this ain't no trap, homie. I don't fuck with that nigga. In fact, he's the reason why I've gotta wear this shit for the rest of my fucking life." He pointed to the hearing aid in his ear.

"What? That Bluetooth?" he asked, confused.

Zekey looked at Montez like he was a fucking imbecile. He then looked up at the sky, talking to God, "Nah, youngin' this ain't a Bluetooth. It's a hearing aid."

Montez angled his head and took a closer look at the device attached to Zekey's ear.

"Oh, my bad," Montez told him and glanced at his watch. "Look, as much as I'd like to keep shooting the shit here, I've got some moves I've gotta make."

"Right," Zekey replied and held up a piece of paper. The address of the house he'd seen KiMani outside of was on it. He extended it to Montez, who was about to take it until he snatched it back from him. "Not so fast, youngsta, I'ma need that payment first." Montez reached into the back of his jeans and pulled out a manila envelope thick with cash. He and Zekey made their exchange.

"Mothafucka's been practically hiding under our noses," Montez said to no one particular. He was familiar with the address on the piece of paper.

Zekey opened the manila envelope and peered inside at the money. He grabbed one of the stacks of dead presidents, dragged his thumb over the top of it, and kissed it. Afterward, he placed the money back inside of the envelope, folded it up, and stashed it inside of his jacket.

"You not gon' count that?" Montez asked as he stuck the piece of paper inside of his pocket.

"Nah, I haven't metta nigga stupid enough to play with mine," Zekey told him confidently. "I'm with all the extras, Blood. I don't care about death or prison! Now, who'd wanna runna foul at a nigga like that?"

Montez's eyebrows slanted, and he smiled devilishly. "Another nigga like that," he stated. This let the older man know he was about the same shit that he was about. "Anyway, I gotta bounce. Good looking out on the info."

"Oh, uh, one more thing," Zekey said as he held up his finger. Montez threw his head back like, *what's up?* "I don't give a fuck what y'all niggaz do to KiMani, but chu leave my nephew alone. You hear me? Y'all leave Arnez be." Montez nodded. "Lemme hear you say it. I needa hear you say it."

"We're going at KiMani, but we're going to leave your nephew alone," Montez said.

Zekey nodded with satisfaction.

Keeping his eyes on Zekey, Montez whistled! Right then, a dark figure dropped from the tree Zekey was posted under, landing behind him. Startled, he whipped around, reaching for his piece, but stayed his hand when Montez told him to relax.

"...See, I told yo' ass I was watching you. I hadda make sure you were one hunnit," Montez told him. "Come on, Abrafo." He motioned for the dark figure to follow him.

As the dark figure walked past Zeke, he took a good look at him. He stood six-foot-three and had a muscular physique. Homie was big and intimidating. He wore body armor over a red muscle shirt that hugged his form and combat boots. He had a big ass Bowie knife with a spiked fist guard sheathed at the small of his back and semi-automatic pistols in his shoulder holsters. Zekey took note of the tribal scars on his arms as well as the ones on his face when he pulled off his ski mask. The scars represented the milestones in his life as well as the tribe he belonged to.

Abrafo (which meant warrior in Ghana, where he was from) didn't bother looking in Zekey's direction when he passed him. He knew his aura made niggaz uneasy, and Zekey wasn't any exception. He could tell by his vibe he was a little shook, which was good. Abrafo wanted him to be mindful not to ever run afoul at him or his boss.

"Abrafo, fuck kinda name is that?" Zekey said as he watched Montez and the foreign hitta disappear into the night. A minute later, he heard a vehicle start up, and seconds later, a navy-blue Chevrolet Tahoe drove by the park. Right after, Quan drove up beside Zekey, and he hopped into the front passenger seat. He slammed the door shut behind him, and she drove away.

***

Two nights later

Though the basement was spacious and well lit, it smelled of dog, death, and blood. This was due to dog fights taking place down here for large sums of money—money made through illegal activities, since there were pimps, gangstas, boosters, and street corner hustlers placing the bets. Although the underground dwelling operated as a dog fighting arena, tonight, it would be used for something very different—a domain for torture.

Boop, wop, wam, bam!

Blood, sweat, and snot flew from his swollen, bruised face as he was kicked and struck with the stocks of automatic weapons. He collided with the cement floor, with snot hanging out of his nose and slimy ropes of blood hanging from his chin. Besides the one blood-stained sock he was wearing, he was naked as the day he was born. Every inch of his body was covered in purplish-blue bruises and blood. On top of that, he was wheezing. It hurt like hell every time he took a breath. Wincing, he sat up on his elbow and held his aching side. Through his one good eye, he took in all of the goons surrounding him. There were four in total. All of the goons were six feet and above. They were buff and tatted up. Their faces were hidden behind ski masks, and they were dressed in all black. Some of them held the chain leashes of pit bulls and M-16 assault rifles, while others just held the assault rifles alone. They watched unflinchingly as their comrades beat the shit out of the poor bastard they'd formed a circle around.

The ones that stood out amongst the masked goons were Hitt-Man and his wife, Niqua. Hitt-Man's old muscle-bound ass was wearing a red beanie and a red Adidas track suit. He was in immaculate shape and looked youthful in appearance. If it wasn't for the fact he had a salt and pepper goatee, you would have sworn he didn't look a day over thirty.

Niqua stood right beside Hitt-Man. She had smooth chocolate skin, almond-shaped eyes, and long, silky hair, which didn't have a strand out of place. Little mama was wearing a black turtleneck, army-green cargos, and black combat boots, looking militant as fuck. Niqua shared a fat ass blunt with Hitt-Man while they watched their goons give old boy a brutal beat down. Every now and again, the chain leash she was holding would jerk from her white, muscular, red-nose pit pull. The frightening beast was barking hatefully at the man being tortured, trying his best to get a hold of him. As a matter of fact, all of the hostile hounds were growling and barking, foaming at the mouth.

"I can't believe yo ass, nigga," Hitt-Man started, having passed the smoldering blunt back to his wife. "I showed yo' ass mad love. I took you outta the cold, set chu up witcho own spot, put money in yo' pocket, and gave you a hustle to feed yo' mothafucking family, and this is how you repay me? By stealing?" He cocked his head to the side and looked at him, narrowing his eyes. He was staring at him like he couldn't believe he had the audacity to steal a dime from him. "How could you ever bite the hand that feeds you, nigga? I looked at chu like a son, you broke my heart, lil' bitch."

"Hitt-man, Blood, I didn't steal nothing from you. Why would I do that when you done looked out for m—" He was silenced by a sudden kick to the stomach that knocked the wind out of him. His eyes bulged and he held himself, spitting more blood on the floor.

"I ain't tryna hear that shit, Papoose!" Hitt-Man said with a scowl, walking around Papoose with his eyes glued to him. He took stock of all the damage his goons had done to him. The young nigga had suffered greatly, but Hitt-Man felt like he hadn't suffered enough. "I was born at night, not last night, mothafucka! What chu take me for?"

At that moment, his cellphone rang and he answered it. "Good. Bring his ass in here," Hitt-Mann said into his cellular before disconnecting the call. A minute later, there was a racket at the basement's staircase. Hot Boy and JayDee were struggling to bring someone downstairs.

"Calm yo' ass down, nigga! You know what the fuck you did, so now you gotta answer for that fuck shit," a heated Hot Boy said.

"Ah, fuck!" JayDee said painfully.

"What happened?" Hot Boy questioned with concern.

"Mothafucka threw his head back and busted my shit," JayDee responded with swelling lips.

"Damn, yo' shit leaking too," Hot Boy claimed, having examined JayDee's bleeding lips.

"Bitch-ass nigga, you gon' pay for that!" JayDee swore. Right then, there was what sounded like a kick and hard tumbling down the staircase. Someone wearing a black pillowcase over their head, with their hands bound behind their back, came into view as they fell down the steps. They reached the floor and slid a little. Hot Boy and JayDee came down the staircase as fast as they could, adjusting the straps of their M-16s over their shoulders. They roughly pulled their hostage upon his feet and walked him over to Niqua. She handed one of the goons the leash to her pit bull and took the hostage under his arm. The hostage put up a fight, whipping his body from left to right trying to get away from her.

"Aw, shit!" Niqua hollered out and looked to her freshly done acrylic nails. The middle nail was broken and bleeding. Wincing, she sucked the blood off it. Her face balled up heatedly, and she kneed him in the stomach. Once he doubled over, she elbowed him in the face and he dropped on his ass. "That's for breaking my fucking nail. I just got these bitchez done." She looked to Hitt-Man. He was angry. He was walking toward her and the hostage, looking like he was about to put hands and feet on his monkey ass. Niqua threw up her hand, stopping him. "It's okay, Daddy. I got this."

"You sure, baby?" Hitt-Man asked, taking her by her wounded hand. Holding eye contact with her, he kissed her hand affectionately. She then rubbed the side of his face and pulled him close, kissing him sensually.

"Yes, I'm sure, Daddy," she cooed, oozing with femininity that could make the toughest of men weak in their knees. She kissed him once more and whipped around to the hostage, pulling out her nickel-plated .45 automatic. Her face balled up with animosity. Just that quick, she transformed into the true gangsta she was, yanking the hostage back to his feet. Once he was standing upright, she stepped back and placed her piece to the side of his dome. "The next time you buck against the queen, I'ma knock yo' ass off the chess board. I'm not the bitch you wanna play with—trust." She lowered her .45, grabbed him under his arm, and thrust him forward. Hitt-Man grabbed him under his arm and walked him into the circle where Papoose was lying. Papoose stared up at Hitt-Man and the hostage, wondering who it was beneath the black pillowcase.

"Look who dropped by to visit us." Hitt-Man smiled devilishly and yanked the pillowcase from the hostage's head, revealing his identity. Assassin stood, narrowing his eyes from the light inside of the basement. He had been in the dark for so long that his sight was sensitive to it. He had two knots on his forehead, one bigger than the other, purple swelling under his left eye, and a broken nose. Blood had slid out of his right nostril and over the duct tape covering his mouth. "Your best bud, Assassin." He held him by the back of his neck. "This lil' nigga had rounded up some goons of his own when my boys found 'em. His whole lil' crew was strapping on body armor and loading up them thangz. Now, my guess is, after my boys had snatched you up, he planned on launching an attack to rescue you."

"Yeah, until we kicked down the doe and splashed their asses!" Hoy Boy chimed in. "To his credit, he took out two of ours, but we wet up the rest of dem toy gangstaz he was with," he said, dapping up JayDee, who had helped him kidnap Assassin.

"Young niggas loyal and with the shits. That's hard to find these days," Niqua added her two cents. "Shit's admirable."

"True indeed," Hitt-Man agreed. "It's just too bad he couldn't be loyal to the home team." He turned to Assassin and snatched the duct tape from off his mouth, causing him to wince. "What chu got to say for yo' self?"

"I ain't got shit to say. You already know what's up." Assassin looked at Hitt-Man fearlessly. "You also know what we did, so let's not play games. If you gon' kill us, then kill us. I'm ready to face the consequences of my actions. Me and my nigga." He spat off to the side. "Ain't that right, Papoose?"

Papoose looked Assassin directly in his eyes. They'd promised each other since they'd been running the streets as little niggaz that when the time came, they'd go out like Gs. Having each other there at the final hour brought them both a level of comfort.

Hitt-Man nodded approvingly at Assassin's stance. He walked over to him, grabbed the back of his neck again, and looked him in the eyes. "I'm proud of you, boy. You did what you did and now you're ready to face your punishment. I salute cho gangsta for real, for real." In a flash, Hitt-Man upped his banga and shot out both of Papoose's kneecaps. Papoose howled in pain and gritted his teeth. His kneecaps spurted blood, splashing on the floor. "Let the pits chew his ho-ass up!"

As soon as Hitt-Man gave the order, the goons let go of their leashes, and the hungry dogs took off after Papoose. Their angry red eyes zeroed in on their next meal, and saliva dripped from their razor-sharp fangs.

"Aaaaaaahhhh!" Papoose screamed at the top of his lungs, causing that little pink thing at the back of his mouth to shake. He threw up his arms to shield his face from the hounds' attack, but his actions would prove to be futile.

"Growwllllll!" One of the dogs bit down on Papoose's wrist.

"Arrrrrr!" A second one sank its fangs into Papoose's other wrist.

Two more of the beasts latched onto either of the young man's ankles. All of the dogs present had a part of the youngsta's body. They were growling and whipping their heads from left to right, trying to rip him apart. He continued to scream! He screamed even louder when another dog bit into his face. It placed its paws on either of his shoulders and yanked back violently, over and over again. The vicious attack caused more and more blood to spill down his face, splattering on his pubic hairs and dick. One more hound appeared and bit down onto Papoose's dick and balls. He yanked and yanked, then whipped his head from side to side. The beast was trying his best to tear the poor kid's jewels from his body.

Hitt-Man, Niqua, and the goons stood around watching without batting so much as an eye. Assassin, on the other hand, couldn't bear to see his best friend being torn apart by the savage animals. He turned his head, but Hitt-Man wasn't having that shit.

Fuck that! He wanted the young nigga to see what happened to those that violated him.

"Nah, nah, lil' nigga, you gon' watch this shit!" Hitt-Man said. He tucked his gun and squeezed the back of Assassin's neck so hard he winced. He turned his head to the brutal assault Papoose was facing, forcing him to watch the bloody carnage.

"Aaaahhh! Aaaahhh! Aaaahhh!" Papoose screamed and screamed as the pit bulls pulled away bloody chunks of him. The one that had bit into his face tore off half of it and munched it down. The one that had latched onto his dick and balls yanked them away from him. What looked like small bloody eggs attached to stringy tissue hung from the severed nut sack. The dog threw his head back and munched them down heartily. Finally, a hound came out of nowhere and sunk its fangs into Papoose's throat. It growled angrily as it crushed his windpipe. Instantly, Papoose went silent. His eyes rolled to the back of his head and blood poured out from where the pit bull's teeth were. The beasts continued to devour his body like it was a full-course meal while everyone looked on.

Assassin's eyes accumulated tears and they spilled down his cheeks. His eyes were glassy and pink. His nostrils were flaring. He clenched and unclenched his jaws repeatedly. He was mad and hurt at the same time. He took in all of the faces present so he could remember everyone. They were all going on his personal hit list, and they'd all be dead! He swore it on his life.

Hitt-Man stepped before Assassin and used his gun to tilt his head upward so he'd be looking at him. He studied his face, watching the tears slide down his cheeks and drip off his chin, splashing on the floor. Assassin held his mad expression while his nostrils flared continuously. He was prepared to go out like Papoose had, if that was to be his fate.

"All this over a bitch that wasn't strong enough to go on living for yo' sake? I hope it was worth your life, son. I truly do." Hitt-Man turned to Niqua and tucked his gun at the small of his back. Holding her by her waist, he tongued her down and then kissed her lips. "Look, I'ma be waiting in the car for you. Gone and pop junior so we can get up outta here," he told her. "I hit up Valencia, and she said she with whatever we're with. If you know what I mean." He smiled nastily, kissed her again, and smacked her on the ass on his way up the staircase. Niqua gave him a fake smile. Although she was down with flipping bitchez with him, she didn't exactly like sharing him with them. The only reason why she went along with having threesomes was to satisfy him, but she'd never tell him that though.

"Get down on your knees!" Niqua ordered Assassin, but he didn't budge. He stared at her defiantly. This infuriated her so much she smacked him across the forehead with her piece. He fell to the ground, bleeding from the side of his forehead. Wincing, he stood back up on his knees and stared up at her. His face was scrunched up and his nostrils were flaring. He was pissed more so at his father than her. It was his bidding that she was doing. "You brought that on yo' self, youngin', I don't repeat myself to anyone!" She then leveled her gun between Assassin's eyes. The young gangsta didn't show any signs of fear. The blood of a G coursed through his veins, so he'd undoubtedly die like one.

"You know, it's funny, granted the situation I'm in, I feel more sorry for you right now," Assassin told her. She narrowed her eyes at him, wondering why he felt that way. He read her expression. "'Cause you're in the same situation my mother was in with my pops. I know your situation like it's my—"

"Aww, fuck what this nigga talking about!" Hot Boy said, frustrated. He didn't want to hear anything Assassin had to say. He wanted him dead and buried so he could carry on with his night.

Niqua went back and forth with Hot Boy. Then, JayDee add-ed his two cents, and then Assassin had a lot on his mind to say. Niqua listened to him for the most part, but once he was done, she opened fire, and left the basement sometime after.

Murder didn't bother her at all!

Chapter Seven
Release day

Hellraiser stood facing OG, holding a wrinkled brown paper bag of his belongings. The old head stood with his hands on his son's shoulders, looking him in his eyes. He had a one-sided grin and appeared to be thinking over how to say what was on his mind.

"My boy's a free man. You can finally go home," OG said jovially. His grin turned into a full-blown smile. "I haven't been this happy since the day you were born."

"You know what would make this day that much better, Pops?" Hellraiser asked.

"What's that?"

"If you were walking outta here with me."

"I know," OG said seriously, giving him a fatherly hug. "Don't chu worry about me though. I'll be all right. You just get out there, get cho family together—take care of them. You get KiMani outta them streets and on the right track. The last thing I want is to see 'em in here with me. You setta good example for 'em, son—teach 'em better than what we were taught. You hear?"

Prison was a revolving door for all of the men in the James family. Running in and out of the penitentiary had become a cycle for them—a cycle Hellraiser was hoping to break with Billion and KiMani. He knew KiMani was breaking bad in the streets, but he was going to do everything in his power to change that once he was released. He didn't want his son to continue to follow down the self-destructive path that he and his father had.

"Yeah, I hear you, Pops."

OG kissed Hellraiser on the side of his head and hugged him tighter, patting him on his back. He then held him at arm's length and told him he loved him.

"I love you, too."

OG's eyes turned glassy as he nodded. He knew he was on the verge of crying, so he slipped his glasses back on, picked up the book he'd been reading, and lay back on his bunk. He held the book in front of his eyes so his son wouldn't see the tears sliding down his cheek. Although he was happy to see his son going home, it was killing him not to be able to go along with him. He wanted to go home to his family and be a grandfather to his grandchildren. He'd written down a long list of things he had in mind to do with them if he was on the outside. In fact, he kept it inside of the book he had in his hands and was looking at it right then.

Hellraiser stared at his father for a minute before walking out of his cell where Corrections Officer Minks was waiting for him. They made their way down the tier side by side. As they went along, Hellraiser exchanged his goodbyes and dapped up the niggaz he knew. Hellraiser and CO Minks made their way across the floor where a mahogany-complexioned kid was mopping the floor. He had a goatee that was in the beginning stages of growing, and he wore his hair in a curly top fade. He had a keloid scar on the side of his neck he'd gotten courtesy of a knife fight while incarcerated. He hadn't gotten the proper medical attention for it to heal properly, so it was as thick as a leech. The kid mopping up the floor had a muscular build, and his knuckles were scarred and calloused.

The kid looked in Hellraiser and Minks' direction, hearing them approaching. He took the mop in both hands and stood upright. A one-sided smile formed on his thick lips, and he threw his head back like, *what's up?*

"Big dog, they're finally lettin' you up outta here, huh?" The kid asked. His honey-brown eyes set off his skin tone and made him irresistible to practically every woman he came across. When homie was free, he was a real lady killa. There wasn't a bitch he couldn't have his way with. He owed it all to his good looks and gangsta demeanor. As cliché as it was, good girls loved bad boys. They couldn't get enough of that thug passion.

"Yeah, Kyjuan, I'm outta here," Hellraiser said. He slapped hands with him and gave him a gangsta hug.

"Good luck out there, homeboy."

"Appreciate that."

"No doubt." Kyjuan nodded.

"Look here, young homie, I needa favor."

Kyjuan looked over his shoulder and saw Minks. He leaned closer and said in a hushed tone. "Yo, you sho' you wanna chop it up in front of ya man behind you?"

"Nah, it's nothing like that, my nigga. I just want chu to look after my old man now that I'm leaving."

"Aww, man, you don't even have to ask," Kyjuan told him. "We done became like brothas in here, my nigga. Yo' pops is my pops. Ain't nothing gon' happen to him that ain't gon' happen to me first."

"That's love."

"Fa sho'."

Hellraiser and Kyjuan dapped up and hugged again. Hellraiser then walked off, waving goodbye to someone on the top tier that was telling him to take care of himself on the outside.

***

Hellraiser emerged from the building he'd been holed up in for the past fifteen years. Immediately, his face balled up from the intensity of the blazing sun. He placed his forearm above his brows to thwart off its bright light.

"Dad, Dad!"

"Babe, hey, hey!"

The voices of Billion and Lachaun drew Hellraiser's attention ahead. He could see their silhouettes as they ran toward him joyfully. A smile stretched across his lips, and his chest swelled with the affection he had for them. Throwing his brown paper bag aside, he took off running to meet them. The closer he got to them, the more their faces filled out and he could see that they were smiling. Everything was moving in slow motion to him. It was as if time had slowed down just for this specific moment.

Hellraiser snatched up his wife and son by their waists. They all laughed as he spun them around in circles. He eventually became dizzy and fell to the ground with them. Time sped back up to its normal pace then. They lay where they were, breathing heavily and smiling. Billion hugged his father around his neck while Lachaun turned his face to her, kissing him romantically.

"I'm so happy you're home, Dad," Billion told his father in his proper voice. He grew up entirely different from his older brother and father. He went to one of the best private schools in Southern California with children of multicultural backgrounds. His institute of learning was far away from the ghetto. The boys were to wear blazers and ties while the girls were to wear blazers and knee-length skirts.

"I'm happy I'm home too," Hellraiser replied with a smile. At this time, he had his arms around Billion and Lachaun's necks, and they were walking toward her car.

"He was so excited that we were coming to get chu that he stayed up all night. You were all he talked about this entire week," Lachaun informed her husband.

"Oh, yeah? Is that right, son?" Hellraiser asked.

"Yep," Billion stated proudly. He loved his father and didn't care who knew it.

"Y'all didn't spill the beans to Ki about me coming home, right?" Hellraiser inquired, looking from Billion and Lachaun.

"I don't know about Momma, but I didn't say anything," Billion said seriously. "Besides, Ki told me never to tell anything on anybody, 'cause stitches get stitches."

"Yeah, that's definitely my son." Hellraiser smiled and shook his head. He then looked to Lachaun. "What about you, lover?"

"Notta word," she assured him. "If I had, you know he woulda been here with us. You know how our oldest is about chu."

"Good. I want it to be a surprise when I roll up on 'em."

"Babe, you forgot to get your bag," Lachaun said, glancing behind her.

"Ah, to hell with that bag," he replied, grinning. "What's most important to me is under these arms of mine." With that said, Lachaun smiled and laid her head on his shoulder, taking hold of his wrist. "Where'd you park?"

"Right there, Dad!" Billion said, pointing at a triple-black luxury vehicle. Its paint job gleamed beneath the sun and reflected a colorful rainbow.

Hellraiser narrowed his eyes and took a closer look at the car his son was pointing at. A fortyish man in a firm-fitting suit stood at the backdoor holding his wrists at his waist. A smile was plastered across his face.

"Nice whip," Hellraiser said, taking in the ebony sedan once they'd gotten close enough. "Did that mixed slave come with it?"

Lachaun laughed and playfully punched Hellraiser. "Babe, stop, don't say that."

"He's not a slave, Dad. His name is Myron."

"Myron is our chauffeur and bodyguard, baby. I thought I told you about 'em."

"You may have, lover," Hellraiser said. "To tell you the truth, I've had so much going through my head while I was caged up I probably forgot it."

"I understand, honey." She kissed him on the cheek. "Well, you're on the outside now. The only thing you have to be concerned with is our happiness. Everything else should be a breeze now that money isn't a concern for us."

Lachaun did exactly what she and Hellraiser had planned while he'd been locked up. The only thing different was, she took it to another level—a level that made them rich beyond their wildest dreams and created generational wealth. Thanks to her making the right investments and their businesses booming, the James family was now multimillionaires.

"Baby, this is our chauffeur and bodyguard, Myron," Lachaun began the introductions. "Myron, this is my hubby, Treymaine James."

"I've heard so much about chu. It's a pleasure to finally meet chu, Mr. James," Myron said with a smile and firmly shook Hellraiser's hand. He was a tall gentleman who was the product of an interracial marriage. He had boyish good looks and wore his naturally curly hair in a mohawk. A scar lay over his left eyebrow and cheek, while another one went across his left jaw. Myron, who was also referred to as "Country Boy" among his company, hailed from Houston, Texas. He was a retired United States Navy SEAL who received the Navy Cross and Purple Heart for his actions in 2005 against Taliban fighters.

"The feeling is mutual, Myron. And please, call me Treymaine or Trey."

"Okay, Trey."

"Yeah, this a bad mothafucka right here," Hellraiser said of the car, licking his lips and rubbing his hands together. He walked around the polished whip, taking in its appearance while seeing his reflection in its body. "What's this, mamas?"

"An Audi A8 Security L," Lachaun stated proudly while she walked around the car with him. She'd had the ride for quite some time, and she was in love with it like she'd purchased it yesterday. "It wasn't supposed to be released until 2021, but I placed a few dollars in the right hands and got it earlier."

"How much she set chu back?" Hellraiser asked, seeing Myron opening the backdoor for Billion. The boy dipped inside of the car and came back out with a tablet.

"$1.25 million." Hellraiser's eyes bulged, and he put his hand on his chest, stumbling backward. He was acting like he was having a heart attack after hearing the price of the automobile. "Hahahahahahaha! Baby, relax, that lil' bit of money didn't fade us. We're straight."

"I wasn't expecting you to say that much," Hellraiser said as he threw his arm over her shoulders and kissed her on the cheek.

"Well, it comes with a lot, babe," Lachaun told him.

"Yeah, Dad, this baby is loaded. Just look," Billion said, standing beside his parents with the tablet. They looked at the device's display, and it had a stunning visual of the exact same model car they owned. Billion tapped the face of the tablet, and the video played. The voice of the narrator, which belonged to an older man with a British accent, gave a description of the classy whip on the screen.

"Audi's armored vehicle has proven popular thanks to its ability to mix a subtle, business-like aesthetic with top-quality safety measures. The A8 L's passenger safety cell is crafted from aramide fabric, special aluminum alloys, and hot-formed steel armor, which offers VR 9 class protection without added weight. Other features include an armored communication box in the luggage compartment, intercom, selective door unlocking, emergency exit systems, fire extinguishing systems, and an emergency fresh air system…"

A six-foot-tall white man looking to be in his mid-to-late thirties walked into the frame. He stood approximately ten feet away from the armored automobile. He was dressed like a mercenary. He was wearing black sunglasses, a tactical bulletproof vest over army fatigues, and combat boots. The strap of an AR-15 was across his broad chest. In his gloved hands, he had a .44 magnum revolver and in the other, a .45 automatic pistol.

"…the Audi A8 has 3.5 inches of bulletproof glass and body armor capable of stopping rounds from virtually any pistol. Here is our assistant, Sergeant Efrem Guile, firing first, a .44 magnum revolver and then a Colt .45 automatic pistol ten feet away."

Efrem opened fire on the Audi with both of the guns, but their bullets didn't pierce it. He holstered the guns and fired his AR-15 from the same distance. The assault rifle only left scratches behind on the exterior of the automobile. The narrator went on about how the Audi was also bomb and grenade proof. Efrem pulled the ring out of a grenade and rolled it underneath the car. He then ran away, ducked, and stuck his fingers in his ears. He frowned, bracing himself for the explosion.

Ka-Boom!

The luxury vehicle barely budged from the impact of the exploding grenade.

The narrator went on talking about the Audi A8, but Hellraiser had heard enough. He had Billion stop the video. They then got into the car and Myron drove out into the flow of traffic.

"So, babe, what do you want to eat for your first meal now that you're a free man?" Lachaun asked as she rubbed the back of his head affectionately. She was looking at him like he was the only man she desired on the face of the planet, and he loved that shit.

"McDonald's," Hellraiser replied.

"McDonald's?" she blurted with a frown. "I thought you were gon' say something other than that. You surprised the hell outta me."

"I've been seeing those commercials for the past two weeks," Hellraiser said. "They got me craving that shit. They've gotta two-for-six special on the Big Mac and the fish sandwich. I want three Big Macs, two apple pies, large fries, and a strawberry shake. I don't want that whip cream and cherry they serving with them now, though."

"Me neither," Billion said while snuggled beside his dad, watching a toy review on his tablet. His eyes were focused on the device's screen.

"Okay. Mickey D's it is then," Lachaun said, and then hollered up front to Myron. "Myron, find the nearest McDonald's please."

"No problem, Mrs. James," Myron said, looking back and forth between the windshield and the screen of the navigation system. "I saw one on our way up here. It shouldn't be too far." He programmed the address to the popular restaurant into the navigation that he'd remembered on the drive up to the prison.

***

Hellraiser, Lachaun, Billion, and Myron ate inside of the restaurant. They chopped it up, laughing and joking over their meals. Once they'd finished eating, they hopped back on the highway. The sun began to set. Billion had fallen asleep leaning up against the passenger door, drooling. He was snoring and his drool had stained his shirt. His mother and father smiled looking at him. Lachaun passed Hellraiser their son's hoodie and he draped it over him. He then kissed him on his forehead and caressed his cheek with the back of his hand.

"My lil' man tired as a runaway slave," Hellraiser said, holding Lachaun's hand.

"I told you he was up all night anticipating seeing you," Lachaun told him. "He even wrote a long list of things he wanted us to do as a family. KiMani included. He loves his big brother. They have a tight bond."

"Speaking of Ki...what's up with him?" Hellraiser asked, wearing a serious expression.

Lachaun took a breath, like she didn't really want to tell him what was up with his oldest son.

"You know how that boy is, babe," Lachaun replied. "Ain't nothing changed. KiMani is out in them streets doing him."

"You mean he's still in the trenches with the life we've built for 'em? That doesn't make no fucking sense," Hellraiser said with crinkled brows. "He's taking penitentiary chances for nothing. I was out in the streets doing the shit I was doing so he wouldn't have to."

"That's exactly what I said, baby, but he wasn't trying to hear that," Lachaun told him. "He said he doesn't want our money...he doesn't needa handout 'cause he's gonna make his own way—like a man. He said he'd rather get it out the mud than be fed with a silver spoon."

"Goddamn fool," Hellraiser said, shaking his head with Ki-Mani in mind. He understood his stance, but felt like he was a fool for not taking advantage of the opportunity that had been afforded to him.

After Big Ma had passed, KiMani went to live with Lachaun, but there wasn't anything she could do with him. She tried her best to raise him right, but she also had a child of her own she had to worry about. KiMani had dropped out of school and started running the streets full time at the age of thirteen. Although he respected Lachaun as his stepmother, he didn't listen to her when she put her foot down. He basically did whatever he wanted. It got so bad that she just said fuck it. She made him promise to eat dinner with her and Billion as a family every night and to answer his cell phone whenever she called him. That way, she knew that he was alive and okay. The arrangement worked out to a young nigga's liking. He kept to his end of the deal even once he moved out of the mansion.

"I'ma have to holler at dude, for real, for real," Hellraiser said. "My main objective now is to put my family back together."

"I feel you, baby, and I got cho back," Lachaun assured him. She then kissed him and laid her head in his lap. She closed her eyes and drifted off to sleep.

Hellraiser played in his wife's hair while staring out of the passenger window. He could see his reflection in the window as he thought about how he was going to go about reaching KiMani. The streets could possess a man like an evil spirit. Therefore, he was going to have to damn near perform an exorcism to get his boy back.

"Whatever it takes..." Hellraiser said with a determined look on his face. "Whatever it takes."

***

As soon as the sun went into hiding, the moon rose high in the sky, sharing its remarkable glow with those fortunate enough to reside in the city of Calabasas. Myron drove the Audi A8 Security L up to the security guard standing at attention at the check-in booth. The security guard recognized Myron. He waved to him and pressed the button that activated the gates of the exclusive community. Myron nodded in acknowledgement and threw up his hand at the security guard as he drove over the threshold. Hellraiser took in his surroundings from the back windows of the luxury vehicle with his fingers interlocked with Lachaun's. She pointed at different mansions, telling him about different celebrities that lived inside of them.

Myron drove up and parked outside of the James' mansion. It was a beautiful $2.35-million-dollar estate sitting on 30 acres of land. It was the most amazing mansion inside the gated community, and Lachaun and Hellraiser were its proud owners.

"Look at my lil' man, he's knocked out cold," Hellraiser said to Lachaun while looking at Billion. He was still asleep, but now he was snoring softly.

"My baby is tired," Lachaun said with a smile, looking over her husband at Billion.

The backdoor being opened took their attention from Billion. Myron was standing outside holding the door open for them to get out.

"Would you like for me to get lil' man and carry 'em in the mansion?" Myron asked, looking from Hellraiser to Lachaun, waiting for their answer.

Lachaun looked to Hellraiser to see what he wanted to do.

"Thanks, but I got 'em," Hellraiser told Myron. "I've been waiting five years to tuck in my lil' man." Myron smiled and nodded understandingly. He then helped Lachaun from the backseat of the car.

Hellraiser got out of the car and looked up at the mansion. It looked the same as it did in the pictures Lachaun had sent him while he was locked up. It fucked him up how what they talked about over the jack years ago had manifested into a reality thanks to their hard work. The crib looked just like they'd envisioned it would. It had everything they wanted besides the four Doberman Pinschers to guard it. But that was okay by him since they lived inside of a well-guarded, gated community and had Myron on deck for any trouble that arose.

Hellraiser went about the task of getting Billion out of the backseat. He hoisted him up in his arms and slammed the door shut behind him. He turned around to see Lachaun disappearing inside of the mansion's door while Myron stood watch at the door. His head was on a swivel as he took in his surroundings, making sure there weren't any lingering threats in his presence. Hellraiser picked up on him looking out for him and his son, and he hurried up the steps. Once he crossed the threshold, he heard Myron shutting and locking the door behind him.

Hellraiser didn't bother asking anyone where Billion's bedroom was located. He knew where it was since the boy had shown him one day while they were video chatting. He made his way up and around the spiral steps, seeing Lachaun disappear inside of their bedroom. Their bedroom was directly across from the one

Billion slept in. Hellraiser entered Billion's bedroom, tossed the sheet halfway off his bed, and sat the boy down. Billion's bowed head bobbled as his father removed his jacket and then all of his clothing. The boy was left in Spiderman underwear. His father laid him down in bed, tucked him in, caressed his cheek, and rubbed the top of his head. Smiling, he kissed him on his cheek and then his forehead.

"Night, night, lil' man," Hellraiser told him before heading for the door. He was pulling the door shut when Billion spoke again.

"I'm so, so happy you're home, Daddy. I love you so much," Billion said groggily.

Hellraiser stopped midway of closing the door and looked over his shoulder at his son. "I'm happy to be home, lil' man. And I love you more than I love anything in the whole, wide world." He waited for Billion's response and heard the sounds of his light snoring. With that, he shut the door behind him and walked towards the bedroom he and Lachaun shared.

"Goodnight, Mr. and Mrs. James!" Myron called out from the floor below. Hellraiser peeked over the guardrail of the balcony. He threw up his hand and bid the bodyguard a good night. Once Myron had exchanged pleasantries with Hellraiser, he walked to the bedroom he'd been assigned to since he'd been hired as Lachaun and Billion's bodyguard.

Chapter Eight

Hellraiser walked up to his and Lachaun's bedroom door. He was about to knock, when Lachaun suddenly snatched it open and pulled him inside. She forced him against the door and came at him like a feral animal, kissing him hard and aggressively. She then tore open his button-down shirt, revealing his chiseled chest and six-pack abs. He snatched the towel covering her water-beaded body and flung it aside. She sucked on his lips, licked up his neck, and used the tip of her tongue to trace his collar bone. He leaned his head back and gasped, feeling her flick his nipples with her tongue. She started sucking on them as she hurriedly unfastened his belt and unzipped his jeans. His jeans dropped around his ankles in a pile. She pulled his boxer briefs down around his hairy thighs and took hold of his piece. She squeezed it and stroked it up and down. It aroused her to feel it growing in length and expanding in her small hand. He was so worked up he was oozing out of his pee-hole, and he hadn't even penetrated her yet.

Lachaun went back and forth between Hellraiser's nipples. She continued to stimulate them, flicking and sucking them while stroking his dick. He moaned and groaned like a little ho as his nipples grew hard.

"My dick hard as fuck, ma," Hellraiser said, looking down at his piece in Lachaun's hand. His forehead was wrinkled and he was licking his lips. "Toppa nigga off, I'm tryna fuck yo' mouth," he told her as he thrust himself in and out of her fist. While he was fucking her grip like it was a pussy, she squeezed her clit and then started rubbing on it. A tantalizing sensation quickly expanded at her kitty. She moaned sexily with her eyes closed and her mouth hanging open. Swiftly, her shoulder moved up and down as she diddled that small flap of meat nestled between her fat coochie lips.

"Aaaah, aaaah, aahhh, oooh, oooh, yes, yes!" Lachaun said, feeling her juices sliding down either of her thighs. Her clit was stiff and so were her nipples. Those shits were poking out like an infant's fingers.

Hellraiser placed both hands on Lachaun's shoulders and continued to fucked her grip. The sounds of his heavy breathing and grunting further heightened her arousal. Her eyes were still closed. Her facial expression went back and forth between a frown and a smile of satisfaction. She could feel her orgasm building, going higher and higher. She gasped and then she became silent. Then she came harder than a bitch, throwing her head back screaming. There was a splash between her legs and what looked like buckets upon buckets of her essence smacked down on the floor.

Lachaun was exhausted and wanted to collapse, but she also wanted to please her man. This drove her to keep it going, which would be easy since she was so riled up and wanted to get even nastier.

"I can't take it—I can't take it no more," Hellraiser said, still humping her grip. She wrapped her other hand around his dick and squeezed it a little more. She wanted him to feel like he was actually smashing her. "I wanna bust—I wanna bust up in yo' mouth!"

Hellraiser snatched his piece from out of Lachaun's hands and forced her down to her knees. Clenching his jaws, he looked down into her eyes, jacking his shit like a maniac. She looked up at him with a wide-open mouth, jabbing her tongue at him. She pinched and pulled on her left nipple while she flicked her clitoris rapidly with her middle finger.

"I wanna—I wanna suck yo' big black dick so fucking bad," Lachaun told him, fluttering her eyes and steadily jabbing her tongue at him teasingly. She moaned sexually to entice him while exciting her ultra-sensitive lady parts. "Put it in my mouth, daddy. Ram that big black mothafucka down my throat! Make me yo' slut! Ssssss, uh, turn me out! Turn me out—goomp!"

Lachaun was interrupted by Hellraiser shoving himself in her mouth. She nearly puked, feeling his pulsating tip at the back of her throat. He maintained eye contact with her as he clutched either side of her head, humping into her mouth like a mad man. Sweat slid down his face and chest, making his skin glisten. He was scowling with squiggly veins pronounced on his temples, chest, biceps, and arms. He was jabbing Lachaun's warm, sloppy mouth with so much intensity that his perspiration dripped from him like a busted water pipe. Droplets of it broke free from his brows and chin, hurtling down below.

"Ack, ack, ack, gag, gag, gag!" Lachaun choked on the end of her husband's meat stick, with tears spilling out of her eyes, and strings upon strings of her saliva oozing out of her mouth. Still, she maintained eye contact with him while continuously manipulating her left nipple and her clit. He couldn't see it, but the beastly way he was attacking her mouth had her busting nuts all over herself. She absolutely loved when he came at her aggressively with his dominating nature. It really got her going and fiending for more.

"Yeah, yeah, that's it, baby! You know how I like that nasty shit!" Hellraiser told her as he licked his lips, fucking her mouth savagely. He could feel his dangling nutsack slapping up against her chin with every feverish thrust. After a while, he started grinding inside of her shit passionately. This made more tears spill from her eyes, more slimy strings of saliva ooze out of her mouth, and more gagging sounds to escape her lips. "You like that shit? Huh? You like it?" Lachaun's eyes were rolled back in her head, and she had a mouthful of her husband's meat. She was busting off crazily and drenching the carpeted floor below her. He didn't know how she did it, but she managed to say 'yes' to what he was asking her with a stuffed grill. "Awww, fuck." He threw his head back and closed his eyes, still grinding between her lips. "I wanna bust, but I don't. Sssssss, I want some of that pussy. A nigga trying to bust a fat ass nut deep down inside yo' sexy ass," he told Lachaun. "Come on, lil' mama, get up there on the bed and spread your legs."

Lachaun spat on the floor and wiped her wet eyes and mouth. Her hair was frizzy and her face was drenched. Her appearance made her look crazier than a shit-house mouse. She rose up off her knees and made her way towards the bed. She wasn't moving fast enough for Hellraiser, so he smacked her on her ass, sending a ripple through it. Lachaun whined, feeling the stinging sensation on her left butt cheek. Shorty was a freak, and she liked it rough. She looked over her shoulder at Hellraiser and licked her lips seductively. Smiling, she stuck out her tongue and made her teardrop ass dance, one cheek at a time.

"I see you've learned a couple tricks since I've been gone." Hellraiser grinned while watching her ass dance. He stroked his dick as he kicked off his underwear and jeans. He walked towards Lachaun, who was crawling onto the bed. She lay on her stomach, making her booty dance to an imaginary beat. Seeing her buttocks moving in such a way drove Hellraiser crazy. His dick grew harder and jumped up and down. As he crawled onto the bed, he licked his lips in anticipation of feeling the heat of her kitty. He straddled her thighs and aimed the tip of his dick at the opening of her shaved vagina. He sunk his piece halfway inside of her, and then he slammed it forward.

"Aaaahhh!" Lachaun hollered in pleasure and pain then started moaning. She came as soon as he slammed into her tightness, and her pussy flooded with her juices.

"Mmmmmmummmmmm," Hellraiser said under his breath and closed his eyes briefly. Lachaun's coochie felt just as good as his freedom. He licked his lips and breathed jaggedly, laying his body on top of her. He used one hand to grip her by her throat while he reached beneath her with the other. He pressed two fingers down on her clit and rubbed it in a circular motion. As he did this, he ground inside of her and slowly began to pick up speed.

Lachaun whined and frowned with her eyes closed. Hellraiser was digging deep in her and hitting that spot. Her pussy was gushing like crazy. Her eyes rolled to the back of her head and her mouth hung open. Veins etched across her forehead and neck. Her face turned a shade of rose petal red while she was getting her shit beat in. Hellraiser was choking her now and hitting her with fast, hard, circular strokes. Sweat poured down his face and back. His eyes were narrowed. He leaned into Lachaun's right ear, talking big shit as he fucked her savagely.

"This my mothafucking pussy! You hear me? Huh?" Hellraiser said, with his hot breath dampening her ear.

"Ack, ack, ack, gag, gag, gag, gag." Tears spilled out of Lachaun's eyes as she was being choked. The veins across her forehead and neck became more pronounced. She looked like she'd been possessed by a demon, with her eyes rolled to their whites. "Yes—yes—I—I hear—hear you!"

"I want chu to understand something. You're mine! I own yo' mothafucking ass!" Hellraiser continued what he was saying. "I own this mouth." He stuck his finger inside of her mouth. "I own this pussy I'm rubbing on! I own this ass, these titties, this pretty ass face. All of you! All of you belongs to me! Now, lemme her you say it!" He grunted louder and louder as he fucked her harder and harder, making the springs of the bed cry.

"You own me, ack, you own, ack—me! Oh, my God. Oh, my fucking God, gag, babe!" Lachaun made the ugliest face ever while she got her brains fucked out! "Don't stop—don't stop, ack, fucking me! Pleeease! Yes, oh—oh, yes, I'm finna cum! I'm finna cum!"

"Where you finna cum, mamas?" Hellraiser asked in a strained voice. His temples and forehead was covered in bulging veins. He was glistening from perspiring. Hot beads of sweat dripped from his brows and made small splashes on Lachaun. They were having that nasty, sticky, hot, sweaty sex. She loved that shit! "Tell daddy where you finna cum!"

"Ack, ack, gag, ack, I'm finna, ack, I'm finna—ack, cum—on yo diiiiiick!" Lachaun drug that last word and went still in Hellraiser's embrace. Her entire body shook from her head down to her pretty little feet. She suddenly went still. She lay where she was, hot, sticky, and glistening from sweat, getting the dog shit fucked up out of her ass.

Hellraiser smirked, seeing he'd damn near fucked Lachaun into a coma. Now that he'd made sure she was satisfied, it was time he got his nut off. With his dick still stuck in her, he sat up and wiped his sweaty forehead. He held her ass cheeks as far apart as he could and drizzled spit on her asshole. He then rubbed the spit in circles on her crinkle, making sure it properly lubricated. Next, he pulled his manhood from out of her vagina and laid its head where the sun doesn't shine. He pushed himself inside of her hole inch by inch, stretching her further and further open. Abruptly, he slammed his dick forward, and Lachaun's head shot up from the bed. She cried out sexually, and her head dropped back to the mattress. Hellraiser, still holding her ass cheeks apart, slowly began to stroke her. Little by little, he opened her up with his gentle thrusts. Once he thought she'd gotten used to him, he started fucking her fast and hard. He squeezed his eyes shut, tilted his head back, and squared his jaws while clenching either of her buttocks.

"Awww, yeah, fuck, yeah!" Hellraiser called out. "This shit feels good, real good!"

He made a face uglier than Lachaun had and pulled his dick out of her ass. He grunted and then hollered while pumping his meat. White rope after white rope of his semen shot out of his pee-hole like silly string. Lachaun felt the warmth of his slimy babies pelting her back and ass. Exhausted, Hellraiser fell over on the side of the bed. He lay flat out with a smile on his face, breathing hard.

"That—was good, babe—I mean—real good," Hellraiser said between breaths. He was waiting to hear Lachaun's response, but she hadn't said shit. He looked at her, and she was asleep, snoring softly. A big smile spread across his face. He kissed her on the cheek and bounced up from the bed. "I still got it." He raised his fists in the air as he walked toward the spacious bathroom, dick swinging from left to right. He got a wet, soapy washcloth and cleaned his wife's back and buttocks.

Hellraiser draped a sheet over Lachaun and kissed her on the cheek again. He showered, brushed his teeth, and put on underwear. He walked into the big walk-in closet and found that Lachaun's clothes and shoes were on one side while his were on the other. He wasn't trying to get snazzily dressed, he just wanted something comfortable to slip on. He winded up settling on a Nike tracksuit and Nike Air Maxes. Once he'd gotten dressed, he turned off the light inside the walk-in closet. As soon as he did, he heard what sounded like a gun being loaded and cocked.

Click! Clack!

Hellraiser's forehead creased, wondering what was going on. He walked out of the walk-in closet and back inside of the bedroom. He was surprised to see Lachaun wearing a black silk robe, standing over the bed. She was standing over an open gun case with a blower at her side. She'd just picked up two fully loaded magazines out of the case when he'd entered the bedroom. Feeling the presence of someone in the room, she turned around to find Hellraiser walking toward her.

"What chu doing with that, baby?" Hellraiser asked, making note of the blower in her hand. It was a fifteen-round .9 mm Beretta.

"Getting it ready for you, hun," Lachaun told him. She out-stretched the banga and the fully loaded magazines to him.

Hellraiser looked at Lachaun's hands like she was holding two King Cobra rattle snakes in them. He didn't know why she was trying to give him a gun when she knew he'd given up a life of violence. He'd made that vow to God in exchange for him allowing Billion to live.

"Ma, I can't take these. Have you forgotten that I made a—"

"I haven't forgotten your vow, sweetheart," Lachaun told him, lowering the gun and magazines at her sides. "But the world you left behind when you went inside is a hell of a lot more dangerous now. There are kids younger than KiMani blowing folks' heads off just cause. I don't wanna see you become a statistic. Our sons need you—I need you. We just got chu back. We aren't tryna lose you ever again," she told him with tears in her eyes. He hated to see her crying, especially on account of him. He figured if he left the crib strapped, then trouble would come looking for him. But if he didn't, then he didn't have to worry about it finding him. Still, he didn't want his wife worried about him while he was gone, so he decided to take the gun and the magazines. "Thank you," she said, wiping away the tears that just descended her eyes. She watched as he tucked the black steel on his waistline and stashed the magazines in his pocket.

"This thang registered?" Hellraiser asked as he wiped the fresh tears that dripped from her eyes.

"No. It's off the books, and untraceable," Lachaun assured him. She pulled him close and hugged him for what seemed like forever. Finally, he broke their embrace and kissed her repeatedly. He told her how much he loved her and continued to wipe away her tears. She told him she loved him too, sniffled, and wiped her drippy nose with the sleeve of her robe. The moment was kindred to a soldier saying his final goodbyes to his wife before heading out to war. "Give KiMani my love, will you?" she called out to Hellraiser as he opened the bedroom door.

"No doubt," Hellraiser said over his shoulder, leaving the bedroom and shutting the door behind him.

***

Arnez pulled into the parking lot of a liquor store and parked in the back, away from all of the other patrons' rides. He and KiMani scanned the parking lot, looking for the vehicle of the person they were supposed to meet, but they didn't see it. KiMani glanced at the digital clock on the dashboard, and looked back up, taking an impatient breath. Having grown tired of waiting, he pulled out his cellular phone and was about to hit up his contact, when Arnez nudged him and pointed to his whip, through the windshield. The vehicle pulled into the row of parking spaces that they were on and parked directly across from them. Once the driver killed his engine and hopped out, KiMani hopped out and made his way over to him.

KiMani's contact was a slender brotha that resembled the British-American actor Delroy Lindo who played Rodney Little in the movie *Clockers*. He was wearing an off-the-rack suit from JCPenney and a three-dollar tie. He was forty-eight years old but had a thick nest of graying hair and matching five o'clock shadow. Although he was a pretty good narcotics detective, he had three kids that didn't respect him, had been divorced twice, and was swimming in debt. He owed most of his problems to his alcohol-ism and his compulsive gambling. In fact, the bag he was about to make with this transaction with KiMani was going toward the lengthy tab he'd run up with his bookie.

After slamming the driver's door behind him, Narcotics Detective Gill Kramer walked to the rear of his Buick LeSabre, taking swigs from his flask. He wiped his mouth with the back of his hand and motioned KiMani over to him.

"Come on, youngsta, beat yo' feet, I don't have all day," Detective Kramer said, clapping his hands hard and rapidly. He was anxious to get a move on with the transaction so he could lay the money for the play on his bookie. He'd promised the old man he'd have a lump sum of cash for him, with an understanding that if he didn't cough up anything, he'd have both of his legs broken. His being an officer of the law didn't mean shit to the people he was dealing with. They made many people in his field of work disappear that he knew personally, so he knew a badge wouldn't stop his persecution.

Detective Kramer slipped his flask back inside his suit and unlocked the trunk of his whip, lifting it up. He looked at KiMani, and he appeared to walking in his direction even slower than before. It was then that it dawned on him that the wildling didn't give a rat's ass what he had going on. No one was going to rush him to do a damn thing. He was stubborn like that.

"It's like that, young blood? Just fuck me and my time, huh?" Detective Kramer looked at KiMani with contempt. At that moment, the youth shrugged nonchalantly and pulled the hood back from over his head so the detective could see his face. As bad as Detective Kramer wanted to pop his young ass in his forehead, toss him in his trunk, and drive around the city looking for somewhere to dump his body, he was going to refrain from following up with those wicked thoughts. Besides having to put up with KiMani's arrogance from time to time, he actually had a pretty good relationship with the boys. He supplied them with the dope they were pushing throughout the ghetto. He'd check it out of the evidence room back at the precinct and replace it with cooking flour. In addition to that, he brokered hits with them for other gangstaz from other territories that needed their opps' heads knocked off. He'd take a percentage and drop the rest of the bag in their laps for them to divide however they pleased.

"Yo, where the merch at?" KiMani asked him, completely ignoring his question. He wasn't in the mood. He wanted to get what he'd hit him up for and get the fuck out of dodge, ASAP.

"I'm getting sick and tired of these young ass mothafuckaz," a frowned-up Detective Kramer complained under his breath as he leaned down inside of the trunk. He grabbed a big duffle bag and passed it to KiMani. He kept a close look out to make sure there wasn't anyone watching them as KiMani unzipped the duffle bag. "Aye, be incognito with that shit. We don't want everyone knowing what we're doing out here," he told KiMani and took another look around them. There were a couple of stray dogs wondering around, a homeless lady pushing a shopping cart full of junk, and a man panhandling. Besides that, their surroundings were scarce.

KiMani pulled out one of the two tan bulletproof vests occupying the duffle bag. He held it up before his eyes like it was a masterpiece painting. His forehead wrinkled, he narrowed his eyes and angled his head. He had a look on his face like something was wrong with the product he'd come to cop.

"Well, damn, boy, what part about being incognito don't chu fucking understand?" Detective Kramer said with frustration dripping from his voice. He took another precautious scan of the area before focusing his attention back on KiMani. He couldn't help noticing the perturbed look written across his face as he lowered the bulletproof vest. "Fuck wrong? You don't like it or something?"

"Man, this a mothafucking pig's vest," KiMani complained as he lowered the bulletproof vest at his side. "I know we'll be looking at some charges or something if we get caught with one of these shits."

"Ain't that about a bitch." Detective Kramer looked at him like he had some nerve. "Lil' nigga, yo' black ass is strapped right now." He lifted up the lower half of his hoodie and revealed the gun tucked on his waistline. KiMani slapped his hand away and took a step back. "You think you won't get some time for carrying that piece?"

"That's different," KiMani retorted. "I treat this bitch like American Express. I don't leave home without it," he regurgitated the famous slogan of the globally known credit card company.

"You know what, boy," Detective Kramer began, screwing the top off his flask. "You are the biggest pain in the fucking ass I have ever had the misfortune of having to deal with." He took the flask to the head, guzzling it. He then lowered his head and wiped his chin again. He stashed the flask back inside its hiding place and took the bulletproof vest from KiMani. He held it against himself as he presented it to the young nigga like a door-to-door salesman. "What you have here is one fine piece of tactical body armor. This baby here is made out of Kevlar, son. Its strong, synthetic para-aramid fibers exhibit high strength and heat resistance. It's also soft and flexible—yet strong"—He knocked on the bulletproof vest—"ultra-high molecular weight, with a polyethylene fiber produced through a gel-spinning process. This bad boy can stop a .44 Magnum and .45 ACP round like that." He snapped his fingers and looked up at KiMani for his approval. The young nigga looked like he was thinking it over, as he held the bottom of the vest and examined it closely. "So, you want it or what?"

"All right, man, I'll take 'em," KiMani reluctantly agreed.

"My man, this is one purchase you won't forget," Detective Kramer said happily as he placed the bulletproof vest back inside of the duffle bag. He then pulled a mugshot out of his suit and passed it to KiMani. The youth's eyebrows slanted and his jaws tightened as he looked the haggard-looking man in the photograph over. He absentmindedly balled his fist tighter and tighter, causing the veins riddling it to bulge off and on.

"This him?" KiMani asked about the man in the photograph.

"Yep. That's what the information inside of the police report says."

Keeping his eyes on the photograph he'd been given, KiMani pulled out a bankroll of dead white men secured by a beige rubber band and tossed it to Detective Kramer. Once again, he scanned the area for anyone that may be watching them. There weren't any eyes on them, so he secured the money in his pocket and slammed the trunk shut.

Detective Kramer glanced at his watch and then addressed KiMani. "Look here, son, I've gotta be going. But, uh, is everything copacetic?"

"Yeah," KiMani nodded, glancing up from the photograph. "We're good. Just tied up in this beef with these fools from around the way, so the hustling done slowed down 'til we knock these ol' busta-ass niggaz' heads off."

"Anything I can do to help the situation?"

"Not unless you gon' pick up a strap and get at these niggaz with us." Detective Kramer looked at him like, *you know I can't do that shit.* "Yeah, that's what the fuck I thought. Anyway, I'm out." He went to walk away, and the detective extended his fist. KiMani looked at his fist then back up into his eyes before reluctantly dapping him up.

KiMani had always felt some kind of way about doing business with Detective Kramer on account that he wore a badge. The way he looked at it, he was a criminal and homeboy was a detective. They were on different sides of the law, so that made them enemies by nature, which was why KiMani felt like he couldn't trust him.

KiMani grabbed the duffle bag containing the police-issued bulletproof vests and treaded back to Arnez's whip, eyes glued to the photograph. He knocked on the trunk of Arnez's ride, and he popped it open for him. After dumping the duffle bag inside the trunk, he hopped into the front passenger seat and slammed the door. His main man cranked up his ride and cruised out of the parking lot.

Arnez looked back and forth between the windshield and what KiMani was looking at. His face scrunched up, wondering what had his sole attention. "Who is that, my nigga?"

106

"The fool that dropped a dime on my pops," KiMani replied.

Tranay Adams

Chapter Nine

"Yo, who the fuck this fool rolling up, Blood?" Arnez asked, clocking a smoke-gray 2015 Mercedes Benz AMG GLE 43 coupe drive up. Assuming the vehicle posed a threat, he discretely slipped his hand underneath his shirt for his blower.

"I don't know," KiMani replied as he narrowed his eyes and took in the sight of the vehicle, "but I'ma 'bouta light that bitch up like a Christmas tree." He mashed out what was left of the blunt and reached for his waistline. At the same time, he threw up gang signs at the approaching car. The Hyundai stopped before him and Arnez. At the exact same time, the youngstaz drew their bangaz and aimed it at the Mercedes Benz. They were about to chop that bitch up until a muscular hand emerged from the driver's window.

"Hold up, don't shoot! It's me!" a non-threatening voice said.

"Who the fuck is me, Blood?" a scowling KiMani asked.

"Yo, father!" the voice responded.

KiMani and Arnez's faces scrunched up, confused, and they exchanged glances. Still training their blowers on the Benz, the youngstaz focused their attention on the foreign vehicle. The passenger door popped open, and a pair of black Air Max 95s touched the asphalt. A calloused hand gripped the door, and a hulk of a man wearing a black Nike tracksuit pulled himself into view. He smiled from ear to ear when he laid eyes on the young men.

KiMani and Arnez lowered their guns at their side when they realized it was Hellraiser. KiMani's eyes became glassy, and a smile broadened his lips. He didn't say a word as he tucked his gun and ran toward his father. He hugged him tightly and buried his face between his neck and shoulder. The sudden show of affection took Hellraiser by surprise. A smirk formed on his lips, and he wrapped his arms around his son, kissing him on the side of his face. He listened to his weeping as he rubbed his back comfortingly, kissing the side of his face once again. He could hear his sobbing and feel the vibration of his body brought on by his emotions.

"I missed you, Pops, man, I'm—I'm so glad you're home," KiMani said between sobs, tightening his hold on his old man.

"I missed you too, son. I'm glad I'm home too," Hellraiser told him. "Our family can finally be complete now."

"I love you, Pops."

"I love you, too."

Hellraiser looked up to see a confused Arnez watching him and KiMani. Arnez had known his best friend for years, and he'd never seen him react so emotionally. He was always a G and showed very little emotion.

"Yo, I gotta take a leak, I'll be right back," Arnez told them. This was his way of giving them time alone. He went to head inside the house but stopped and turned around like he'd forgotten something. "Oh, yeah, by the way, welcome home, big homie."

"Thanks, Arnez." Hellraiser smirked.

Arnez tapped his fist to his chest and continued toward the house. His cellphone rang as he vanished through the front door, and he answered the call.

"My bad, Pops, a nigga all emotional and shit—crying like a lil' ol' bitch," KiMani said, bowing his head, sniffling and wiping his eyes.

"Hey, hey, hey," Hellraiser said, placing his hands on his son's shoulders. He tilted his chin up so they'd be at eye level. "There's nothing to be ashamed of—even gangstas cry."

"They do?" KiMani asked curiously, forehead wrinkled. He thought Gs were supposed to be hardcore and show little emotions, if any at all.

"Of course they do. I cried many nights behind those walls, son," Hellraiser told him. "Many nights."

"Really? Why?" KiMani's forehead wrinkled further. He wondered what drove a man as gangsta as his father to tears.

"Being away from my family, my sons, my babies," Hellraiser replied. "The fact that y'all were out here in this coldhearted world alone without me to protect you and give you guidance. There wasn't a day that I was in that cage that I wasn't worried about you, your brother, or your mother. Son, believe me when I tell you that I love y'all immensely. And now that I'm here, I wanna try my best to make up for lost time with y'all. You with it?" He grinned and outstretched his fist to him.

"Yeah, I'm with it." KiMani smiled and dapped him up. Hellraiser pulled him close with one arm and kissed him on top of his head.

"You notta shame to have your old man kiss on you? I know you gotta gangsta image to uphold."

"Nope," KiMani replied. "I don't give a fuck what niggaz gotta say. My gangsta certified in these streets. Niggaz betta know this ain't that."

Hellraiser chuckled and said, "Sho' you right."

"On some for real shit, Pops, I got something I want chu to have," KiMani said with a serious expression.

Seeing how serious his son was looking made Hellraiser take on a more serious look. "What chu got?"

"It's in the house. Follow me." KiMani motioned for him to follow him. They went up into the house, closing and locking the door behind them. "I'll be right back, Pops. Grab yo'self something to drink. There's a few Heinekens in the fridge," he said as he disappeared down the hallway.

"Nah, I'm straight, son," Hellraiser replied. He stood at the center of the living room, taking in the décor. KiMani's spot was pretty much what he'd expected for a young man's home to look like. A big-screen television set mounted on the wall, black leather furniture, a stereo system, and a shelf with portraits of him and his family. One particular portrait caught his eye was of him holding a two-year-old KiMani, kissing him on his cheek. Hellraiser smiled at the portrait, recalling that day. He missed when KiMani was that small.

Although Hellraiser wasn't impressed with the layout of KiMani's crib, he was definitely surprised by the religious pictures and crucifix hanging on the wall, and sitting on the shelves. Upon seeing this and the gold rosary KiMani wore around his neck, Hellraiser knew that his son believed in something greater than himself, and was submissive to it. He had Lil' Saint to thank for that, since he was the one to hip him to the gospel. Though Hellraiser wasn't exactly religious, he was grateful for anything that could possibly pull his baby boy out of the streets.

There may be hope for Ki yet, Hellraiser thought as he continued to take in the religious decorations in the living room.

"Well, it's on then, Blood. Lemme holla at my pops and we're gon' start getting ready," KiMani said from the bedroom. Shortly, he returned to the living room with the file Detective Kramer had given him. "Here, Pops."

"What's this?" Hellraiser asked with a creased forehead.

"Take a look," KiMani replied, looking over his father's shoulder as he opened up the file.

Hellraiser's eyebrows dipped and his nose wrinkled the moment he opened the file. He was faced with a picture of the busta-ass nigga that testified against him in court, Elgin. On the spot, his mind was hit with a barrage of images of him shackled down in court, Elgin pointing him out, the judge insulting his character, and then the loud slam of the gavel, which echoed throughout the courtroom and the theater of his mind.

"You know who this is, right?" KiMani asked, looking from the mugshot of Elgin to his father.

"Yeah, I know who this is. I know exactly who this is," Hellraiser replied. He was hot as fish grease and wanted revenge, but he remembered he renounced violence. And to go out looking for blood would lead to him breaking the vow he'd made to God Almighty.

KiMani's face was twisted in hatred and his nose was flaring. "I was gon' smash this bitch-ass nigga myself, but I figure I'd wait 'til you came home and we could ride down on 'em together. You know, a father and son tag team laying our gangsta down."

Hellraiser closed the file and took the time to calm himself down. He shut his eyes and took a deep breath, passing the file back to KiMani. KiMani frowned, wondering what was up with his father's sudden change in mood.

"Son, you mind if I use your restroom?" Hellraiser asked.

"Yeah, Pops, it's straight down the hall, to your left," KiMani told him. Hellraiser headed towards the hallway but turned around when his son called after him. "You good?"

Hellraiser nodded and said, "Yeah, son, I'm straight." He disappeared down the corridor, thinking of how he was going to break the news to KiMani that he wasn't about that life anymore.

KiMani tossed Elgin's file onto the coffee table and headed into his bedroom. He found a bare-chested Arnez standing over his bed, which had assault rifles, pistols, knives, and grenades on it. There were also the bulletproof vests they'd copped from Detective Kramer among the collected items.

"Yeaaah, it's time to serve this fool." KiMani smiled wickedly as he rubbed his hands together in anticipation. Arnez had told him he'd gotten a call from this broad he'd been fucking with for a while who'd also been dealing with Assassin. Little mama gave him the down low on all of the spots homeboy was known to frequent. Arnez committed the intelligence to his memory and relayed it to KiMani as soon as he and his pops came inside the house.

"You goddamn right, Blood," Arnez said, holding a bulletproof vest in one hand as he dapped him up. He slipped the body armor over his head and strapped it to his body. He put on a black T-shirt, black hoodie, and tucked a black bandana into his right back pocket. Lastly, he pulled on a pair of black gloves and flexed his fingers inside of them.

"After we lay out Assassin, Montez, and that supersized African nigga they be running with, the last nigga we gotta worry about is Hitt-Man," Arnez said, smacking on a black LA fitted cap and adjusting it to his liking. While he was doing that, KiMani was strapping on a bulletproof vest and getting ready for the mission they were going on. "We catch his big brolic ass slipping and knock his mothafucking head off."

"What about that broad he be rolling with? Nicki or Niqua," KiMani said, pulling a pair of black gloves over his hands and flexing his fingers in them.

"That's Niqua. Bitch 'pose to be the nigga's wife," Arnez said. "I don't give a fuck. I'm not sexist over here, hoes can get it too. You feel me?"

"Hell yeah." KiMani dapped him up.

"You know what's crazy though, Blood, you gon' trip off this."

"What's that?"

"That bitch looks a lot like yo' moms, except she's thick as fuck, with much longer hair."

"I wouldn't know. I've never seen this ho," KiMani admitted. "But I'll tell you what, if this tramp looks like my moms like you say she does, it's gonna make it that much easier to blow the bitch's face off," he said as he loaded up two FN 509 pistols and laid them on the bed. Next, he picked up a Draco and attached the one-hundred-round drum to it. Gripping it with both hands, he lifted it up and aimed it at a lamp sitting on the nightstand across the bedroom. He imagined himself blowing away Hitt-Man, Assassin, and the rest of them bitch-ass niggaz.

"Run with us or run from us, baby," Arnez said as he started loading shells into the magazine of a machine gun. He and KiMani were so engrossed in what they were doing, they hadn't noticed Hellraiser turning the corner entering their bedroom.

KiMani felt a presence behind him and turned around to his father. A smile spread across his lips, and he picked up the two FN 509 pistols he'd loaded previously. He outstretched them to his old man, and he took them. His forehead crinkled as he held the guns.

"Aye, Pops, this is the perfect time for you to be outta the pen," KiMani told him excitedly. "Since me and Arnez got our own thang popping, we've been bumping heads with Hitt-Man and nem over territory. So, I was thinking since you home now, you can call up some of them old niggaz you used to run with back in the day. We can join forces and annihilate these mothafuckaz!" He scowled and slammed his fist into his palm for emphasis. "Once they're outta the picture, the game is ours, Pops. We'll own the night, but more importantly, we'll own these streets," he said confidently as he placed his hand on his father's shoulder. He was looking at the guns he'd given him like he didn't know what to do with them. Those shits may as well have been a couple of ray guns from outer space.

"I'm sorry, son. But that ain't me no more," Hellraiser regretfully informed him. He flipped the FNs over in his hands so he'd be holding their barrels. He held them up so KiMani could take them. KiMani angled his head and looked at his father through narrowed eyes. He then looked over his shoulder at Arnez, who was still loading up ammo. He made a funny face and shrugged.

KiMani took the FNs from his father and lowered them at his sides. He couldn't believe his ears. He swallowed his spit and took a deep breath.

"Yo, what chu mean this ain't you no more? You're OG Hellraiser from RTBG!" KiMani said heatedly. "Yo' rep is written in blood. You've gotta body count past my mothafucking age. Now you telling me you done hung up yo' guns? What type of shit is that?"

"It's like I told yo' stepmother, son, when I was in prison, and she'd given birth to Billion. I made a vow to—"

"Mothafuck that dumb-ass vow!" KiMani spat aggressively. His forehead was furrowed and his nostrils were pulsating. The young nigga was on one!

"Yo, Ki, chill out. That's yo' father, show 'em some respect," Arnez advised him.

"Stay the fuck up outta my business, Arnez, this between me and my old man!" KiMani told his right-hand man from over his shoulder, then focused back on his father. "Like I said, Pops, fuck that vow you made! You can't be worried about what the fuck is going on up there heaven. You gotta be worried about what's going on down here in hell. This beef we got going on ain't just over drug territory. This fool, Assassin, and his people are killaz! They're head hunting out here, dog! Should they ever catch me, Arnez, or any of the homies slipping, they're not gonna think twice about chopping us down!"

Hellraiser took a breath and ran his hands down his face. He folded his arms across his chest and then he spoke again. "Look, son, I hear what you're saying. You're inna life or death situation, it's kill or be killed."

"You goddamn right." KiMani nodded. "We gon' try to get these niggaz before they get us."

"Onna set," Arnez chimed in as he put the magazine he'd been loading into a machine gun. After he cocked it, he laid it back down on the bed and holstered the pistols he'd previously loaded up.

At this time, Hellraiser was massaging his chin and pacing the floor. He was weighing the options he had in this situation. Coming to a conclusion, he stopped and turned around to his son.

"Look, maybe I can call for a sit-down and we can come to some understanding with Hitt-Man and his people."

As soon as he said that, KiMani bowed his head and shook it shamefully. He was highly disappointed with his father. He was expecting him to be ready to wild out. Although he knew about him making the vow he had, he thought things would be different once he'd finally gotten his taste of freedom.

"I know you not tryna hear that, Ki, but you don't have to be out here in the streets." Hellraiser tried to reason with him. "Your stepmother and I our millionaires—we're rich! We've gotta 'nough money to change your life and your friend's life." He nodded to Arnez, who was holding the machine gun at his side. "You'd do better leaving these streets to the wolves. Let them—"

KiMani appeared to snap upon hearing that. He threw his head up and shoved one of his guns in his father's face. His eyes were red and tears were sliding down his cheeks. His blood was boiling hot. It felt like lava was rushing throughout his veins.

"Wolves? You wanna talk about some mothafucking wolves?" KiMani spat heatedly. "Nigga, I'ma wolf! Me and my niggaz, we're the mothafucking wolves! And you..." He looked his father up and down like he disgusted him. The look on his face said he wanted to vomit. "I don't know who the fuck you are."

"I'm your father, Ki," Hellraiser said, staring him in his eyes. The gun held at his face didn't bother him one bit. This wasn't the first time he'd been at the mercy of one, but he hoped it would be his last.

"Nah." KiMani shook his head as he wiped his tears. "You ain't my pops, my old man issa G. I've been waiting fifteen years for my pops to come home, but yo' bitch ass showed up. I don't know who the fuck you are."

Hellraiser's eyes instantly became glassy. What his son said hurt his heart. He thought he'd never live to see the day any of his children would come at him with such disrespect. The man he used to be would have disarmed KiMani and snapped his fucking neck for his lack of respect. He didn't have that vigor in him right now, though. So he began to think that maybe his boy was right. Maybe he had changed! Maybe he had become soft!

"As a matter of fact," KiMani said, biting down on his bottom lip. "I should just take yo' ass off yo' feet so I won't have to deal witcho weak ass later."

"Go ahead, son, I've seen everything and I've done everything in this lifetime," Hellraiser said unflinchingly. "I'm curious to find out what's popping in the next." He stepped forward and pressed his forehead against the barrel of his son's FN 509. The tears flowed fluidly down KiMani's cheeks as he contemplated blowing his father down. He placed his finger on the trigger and slowly applied pressure to it. All the while, he bit down harder and harder on his bottom lip, trying to find it within himself to do the unthinkable.

Arnez stood in the background, looking between Hellraiser and KiMani, wondering what would happen next. There was sweat peppered over his forehead and some had even slid down the side of his face. He wanted to intervene in the situation, but he was afraid that KiMani would accidently pop his old man if he did. All he could do now was wait to see what would be the outcome of this situation.

"Aaaaaah, I can't." KiMani snatched the gun away from Hellraiser's forehead and walked away from him. He and Arnez went about their business, loading their weaponry up into their gun cases. Once they were done, Arnez walked out of the bedroom

117

with KiMani bringing up the rear. KiMani was the last one out of the bedroom. He stopped inside of the hallway and took a look at his old man, from over his shoulder.

KiMani and Hellraiser held each other's gaze. They didn't know what to say, so there was a long silence between them. Hellraiser's heart was pumping love while his oldest son's was pumping hatred for a father he wasn't sure he knew anymore.

"You may have distain for me, but hopefully we can get past this," Hellraiser told him, placing his hand on his shoulder. "I know I've been gone a long time, but I'm willing to do everything I can to start repairing our relationship. Counseling, therapy— whatever we need to fix this family, I'm down for it. I love you, son."

"I love you, Pops," KiMani replied with a hard face. "Be sure to relay that message to my father when you run into 'em— whoever the fuck you are." He looked Hellraiser up and down in disgust again. Scoffing, he turned his nose up at him and contin- ued down the hallway.

Hellraiser leaned up against the doorway and stared at the floor. He started thinking that maybe KiMani was a lost cause and he should move forward with those who were ready to be the family he had in mind.

Nah, fuck that, I'm not finna give up on my boy. Ki's my blood. This shit is not gonna be easy, but I'ma turn him around somehow, Hellraiser thought, narrowing his eyes and massaging his chin. He was thinking of a way he could appeal to KiMani's logical sense. He tried thinking of how he'd want a fatherly figure to come at him if he was a hotheaded street nigga that believed he knew everything. "Hmmm." He massaged his chin harder until he came up with something. He bolted down the corridor to catch up with his son before he could leave to claim the lives of God only knew how many. "Ki, Ki, Ki!" he called out over and over again, making fast tracks through the hallway.

Blocka, blocka, blocka, blocka, blocka, blocka!

A rush of gunfire woke up the silent night. It stopped for a split second and then continued again.

Blocka, blocka, blocka, blocka, blocka, blocka!

Hearing the semi-automatic gunfire caused Hellraiser's eyes to widen and his heart to quicken. He feared for the worst and prayed for the best possible outcome for what lay before him when he came outside.

The sound of a van speeding off the block filled the air.

Hellraiser unlocked the front door and swung it open. The first thing he saw was an Astrovan covered in sun burns. He looked to the ground where he found Arnez and KiMani lying. His eyes widened further, and his mouth hung open in shock. Arnez was lying still and appeared to be bleeding badly. KiMani lay with both of his FN pistols in his hands. He was wincing and kicking his right leg in agony. The slugs he'd gotten hit with were hot and caused smoke to rise from his body.

"Oh, God, no! No, no, no, no!" A worried Hellraiser leaped from the top of the porch and landed on the ground, taking off towards his son. He kneeled down to him and could see he'd indeed caught fire. With two forceful tugs, he tore the hoodie off him and revealed the bulletproof vest he wore underneath. The vest had stopped three of the slugs sprayed at him, but two were able to penetrate his armor. KiMani wheezed and gasped for breath. There were tears coming out of his eyes from the pain he experienced from getting hit.

"Is it bad? Is it bad, Pops?" KiMani said as tears continued to pour from his eyes. He clenched his jaws to combat the excrucia-tion and tried to look at himself. He managed to see bleeding holes in him. "Ahhh, fuck! Yeah, it's bad, it's bad!" he said, allowing his father to pull off his glove and hold his hand. He could feel him kissing it. When he looked at him, he saw the tears in his eyes and knew he was on his way out.

"You're gonna be fine, son, just fine! You just hang in there okay? Hang in there," Hellraiser told him as he pulled out his cellular and dialed 9-1-1. He told the dispatcher what had occurred and gave them an address. Then he disconnected the call. "Hey, hey, hey!" He smacked his crying son's face to get his attention. He could tell from his eyes that he was on the verge of passing

119

out, and that wasn't good. He knew that if he allowed him to faint, he wasn't going to wake up again. "Look at me, son, you look at me! You're not gonna die, okay? Say it with me now. I'm not gonna…" Hellraiser and KiMani said what he suggested over and over again. As they continued to say it, the police car sirens and ambulance sirens consumed the air.

"Pop—Pops—I'm—I'm sorry for what I said earlier, man. I—I didn't—" KiMani tried to finish, but his father cut him off.

"Shhh, shhh, shhh," Hellraiser hushed him with teary eyes, kissing his hand again. "Don't worry about alla that, okay? It never happened. You hear me? It never happened. Lemme hear you say it."

"It—it never happ—happened," KiMani stammered, fighting the urge to close his eyes.

"That's right. It never happened," Hellraiser assured him, keeping eye contact with him. "Now, I want chu to concentrate on staying awake and alive. 'Cause once you pull through this, we're gonna make up for lost time. You hear me, son? I'm gonna make up witchu by doing all the stuff we never got to do when you were a lil' boy."

"T—tell me, Pops. Tell me what we're gonna do once I get outta the hos—hospital," KiMani stammered again.

Hellraiser swiped away the tears that threatened to drop from his eyes, sniffled, and took a deep breath. "I'm going to take you to your first Laker game—"

"Floor seats?"

"Yep, floor seats." He nodded. "We'll be so close, King James will get some of his sweat on us."

"Where—where else we're gonna go, Pops?"

"The Santa Monica Pier. We're gonna drive the bumper cars, ride the Ferris wheel, play the arcades—"

"And eat—eat cotton candy."

"Lots and lots of cotton candy," Hellraiser promised, still holding his hand.

"Aye, Pops, maybe—maybe we can—we can go to the gun range."

"Boy, you'd think after this shit you'd wanna stay away from guns," Hellraiser said laughing. KiMani laughed right along with him.

"Ahhh, shit, man, don't make me—don't make me laugh," KiMani told him, wincing between laughter. "It hurts—it hurts to laugh, Pops," he admitted as tears spilled out the corners of his eyes, dripping off the sides of his face.

"Aww, fuck!" a serious face Hellraiser blurted.

"What—what is it, Pops?"

"I've gotta get this vest off you and hide these guns."

"Okay, get—get Arnez's too."

Hellraiser glanced at Arnez, who wasn't breathing. He was sure he was dead. Looking back at his son, he bowed his head and crossed himself in the holy crucifix. At that moment, KiMani knew that he'd lost his brother and best friend. The tears flowed constantly from his eyes until he shut them and lowered his head back to the ground.

"Damn, damn, damn," KiMani said over and over again, throwing his head back against the ground just as many times. He felt like he had to survive now in order to avenge his right-hand man's death.

Hellraiser removed the police-issued bulletproof vest from his son's body. He grabbed his guns and ran inside of the house to hide them. If One Time arrived and found him wearing the vest and holding the guns, they'd lock his ass up. That's if he survived the shooting! When Hellraiser ran back out of the house, he found some EMTs putting KiMani on a gurney. He didn't look like he was breathing as they rushed him to the open doors of the ambulance.

Hellraiser stood where he was, frozen in shock as tears slid down his cheeks. The red and blue lights of the emergency vehicles shone on him as he wondered if he'd lost his son for good. One detective was hunched down over Arnez's body while another one was approaching Hellraiser. He whipped out a small notepad and flipped it open. Afterwards, he introduced himself to him and stuck out his hand.

"I'm Detective Mackie," the detective told him. Seeing Hellraiser wasn't responsive, he lowered his hand to his side and started asking him questions about the shooting. Everything he was saying was going in one ear and out of the other. After a minute, he was just talking, because Hellraiser didn't hear a damn thing. He was lost in the fact that he may lose his son to the same streets he'd laid claim to.

Chapter Eleven

The surgery to remove the bullets out of KiMani was a success, but the amount of blood he lost led to him being in a coma. The doctor and his team had done everything they could for him. Now he lay in his hospital bed hooked up to an IV, a few patches to monitor his vitals, a morphine drip, and he was given a blood transfusion every so often to replace the plasma he'd lost from being shot. Now God had to decide whether or not he was going to come out of his coma or not.

KiMani's room was dark and quiet except for the noises the medical machinery was making. His younger brother, Billion, was cuddled up beside him asleep and hugging a teddy bear he'd brought along to keep his big brother company. Sitting across from his bed were Hellraiser and Lachaun. Her eyes were pink and there were dried tears on her face. She'd spent the past few hours sobbing over KiMani's unfortunate circumstances and praying to God Almighty he'd make a full recovery. On top of her stepson's life hanging in the balance, the James' family had lost one more member—Arnez. Although Hellraiser didn't know the young man as well as everyone else, his death was sad and a crying shame. He knew KiMani could have easily been in his shoes, but he was thankful to the Most High he wasn't.

Lachaun and Billion, on the other hand, were hurt, angry, and sad after losing Arnez. To them, he was as much family as KiMani was, and now that he was gone, there would always be a void in their lives.

Hellraiser and Lachaun sat beside each other with their fingers interlocked. Lachaun's head was lying against his shoulder and a hospital blanket was draped over her. She'd been up all day and most of the night, so she was struggling to keep her eyes open. All her worrying and crying had taken a toll on her, and she desperately needed rest.

"I love you, baby," Lachaun told Hellraiser.

"I love you too, ma," Hellraiser replied as he caressed her hand with his thumb. "I know without a shadow of a doubt, if I hadn't had you by my side, I never woulda made it through all the shit I've been through."

"You got my back and I got yours," she told him as he kissed her hand.

"Forever and ever?" Hellraiser asked.

"Forever and ever," she replied and closed her eyes. Before Hellraiser knew it, she'd fallen asleep, snoring softly.

"Man, my wife tired as hell," Hellraiser said, looking at his better half. He kissed the top of her head and scooped her up in his arms. He carried her to the opposite side of the room where there was a vacant bed. After lying her down, he draped the blanket over her. He took two steps before she called for his attention.

"Baby, where are you going?" Lachaun asked faintly.

"To getta soda, I'll be right back."

"Okay. I love you."

"I love you, too," Hellraiser said before continuing out of the room.

***

Hellraiser hopped on the elevator and took it down to the lobby. He entered the cafeteria and made his way to the soda vending machine. He looked down the row of listed beverages the machine offered until he found one he wanted. He reached inside of his jacket's pocket for some loose change and winded up pulling out a gold rosary. It belonged to KiMani. He'd taken it from around his neck before he was whisked away to surgery. Hellraiser switched hands with the rosary and took the change out of his pocket. He dropped three quarters into the soda machine and selected a Pepsi. A moment later, there was an eerie grumble, and a blue soda can dropped to the bottom slot of the machine.

Hellraiser picked up the Pepsi and walked away, cracking open its lid. He guzzled some as he headed back towards the elevator, caressing the rosary with his thumb and thinking of KiMani. Visuals of them having fun when he was a boy played within the theater of his mind, and a smile emerged on his lips.

Ding!

The elevator chimed as it arrived on the floor KiMani was located on. Hellraiser frowned, not realizing he boarded the elevator, and pressed the button for his designated floor. He reasoned he must have been so wrapped up in his reminiscing that he didn't remember his actions. Once the doors parted, Hellraiser made his way out and made a left at the corner of the hallway. As soon as he turned, he saw a balding white priest in a black and purple clergy robe. He was leaving out of the hospital's chapel, closing and locking the doors behind him. After he'd locked the doors, he kissed two of his fingers and placed them on the large wooden crucifix on the door. He playfully tossed the keys in his hand and walked in Hellraiser's direction.

The priest greeted Hellraiser with a nod and pleasant smile as they crossed paths. Hellraiser returned the gesture and continued on his way. He stopped at the crucifix that was hanging on one of the doors of the chapel, and he recalled the vow he'd made to God.

Father, I throw myself at your feet and plead for mercy. I swear that if you spare my child's life, I'll renounce violence in any form. I vow to change my life for the good! I swear on it! If I am lying, may you strike me dead with a bolt of lightning! Amen!

Hellraiser closed his eyes and bowed his head. His mind was assaulted with visuals of him comforting KiMani as he lay bleeding on the ground. The thought of losing his oldest son was overwhelmingly sad and hurtful. He absentmindedly clutched the rosary in his hand tighter. Veins bulged in his fist, neck, and forehead, and his nostrils flared. He looked back up at the crucifix, scowling with pink eyes and tears sliding down his face. He clenched his jaws so hard it felt like his teeth were about to break.

"Look, I know what I promised you, but things have changed," Hellraiser began. "They changed the moment these nigg—these men gunned down my son and his best friend. Now, someone messing with me is one thing, but when it comes to my babies—my family—that's where I draw the line, and blood has to answer with blood." He swallowed his spit as tears continuously flowed down his face. "Whatever punishment that awaits me for breaking my vow, I'll gladly accept it, but as for now, I suggest you make preparations for the souls I'ma 'bouta to send you."

Hellraiser pocketed the rosary as he walked down the corridor drinking his Pepsi. He finished it by the time he returned to KiMani's room and deposited it in the trash can. He scooped Billion out of the bed with his brother and laid him down in the other bed beside his mother. Once he covered him up with her blanket, he caressed his forehead and kissed him. He brushed Lachaun's hair out of her face and kissed her on the cheek. Afterwards, he walked over to KiMani's bedside and rubbed his hand soothingly.

"I promise you, son. I'm going to get those responsible for this," a scowling Hellraiser swore, clenching his jaws. "Every mothafucka involved with your shooting from the shooters to the higher-ups that okayed the hit is gonna get it. That's my word." He rubbed KiMani's hand a while longer and kissed his cheek. "I love you, son."

Hellraiser walked out of the room, pulling his cellphone out of his pocket. If he was going to make a move against the killaz that came at KiMani and Arnez, he was going to need a pack of wild dogs behind him. He knew just the niggaz he needed to get at for his situation. Although they were all retired, he knew they'd come back out if he made the request.

"Yo, Saint, some shit went down tonight, loved one," Hellraiser began as he approached the elevators. "Yeah, I'll let chu know all about it once we link up. Right now, I'm putting outta OG call. I need every gangsta we rolled with back in the day to meet me at my son's crib. That's all I can say over this jack. Make it happen, Blood."

Hellraiser entered the elevator. Its doors closed as he disconnected the call.

***

Lil' Saint, Julian, and Mack were all gathered inside of KiMani's kitchen. Hellraiser had just told them everything that had gone down that night. They all loved KiMani and had a hand in raising him. So, to find out that someone tried to kill him made them thirsty for blood. They were all eager to exact revenge and see to it that the shooters were brought to street justice. The four men chopped it up among themselves as Hellraiser popped the caps of beers and passed each of them one. As they took the occasional swig of their ice-cold brews, Hellraiser took in their numbers. He wasn't particularly satisfied with the turnout, but he'd have to make do. He was sure every man accounted for was battle tested and had a skillset when it came to murder.

"Man, us three are all we have to work with?" Hellraiser said as he leaned up against the kitchen counter with his beer resting against his chest.

"Yeah, man." Lil' Saint looked around at everyone. "This is it."

"What chu see is what chu get," Julian told him.

"I thought we'd have a fifteen to twenty turnout at minimum," Hellraiser admitted before taking a swig of his beer. "Where are all the homies at these days? Wild Kat, Fishbone, Nut, Swamp Thang, Murda, Big Tim, Dawg, Man Man, LaFonze, where them niggaz at?"

"Blood, most of the homies you named are either smoked out, doing a shit-load of time, or dead," Mack informed him.

At the mention of this, Julian and Lil' Saint bowed their heads and crossed themselves in the sign of the holy crucifix.

"God bless the dead," Julian said.

"Damn." Hellraiser took a swig and shook his head. He hated to hear about his fallen comrades. They were all standup niggaz and held the set down while they were running the streets.

Mack walked over to Lil' Saint and Julian and hung his arms around their shoulders. They continued to take the occasional swig of their beers as if he wasn't even there.

"Yeah, this is it here, Blood." Mack looked over their crew. "The Last of the OGs."

"I can drink to that." Julian held up his beer. They all touched bottles and said all together, 'To the Last of the OGs,' and took another swig of their brews.

"So, fearless leader, what's our first move?" Mack asked Hellraiser, who was looking through Elgin's file.

Hellraiser removed the photo of Elgin from the file and held it up for them to see. His face balled up angrily, and he said, "We move on this fool tonight."

***

Elgin sat on a beat-up, old burgundy couch with springs and cotton hanging out of it. His hair was thinning and he had a nappy salt and pepper beard. His eyes were yellowish, his face was covered in blisters, and his arms and hands were swollen and covered in scabs, some of which were bleeding from his scratching. Elgin looked like something out of a fucking horror flick. If the flick had a name, it would be called *Night of the Living Dopefiends!*

Elgin didn't give two fucks about his appearance. He was happy he'd finally gotten what he'd been scraping together money to buy all that day: heroin. The old dopehead loved boys like a Catholic priest. The proof of that was he'd done something that he'd never thought he'd do to get it. He exchanged sexual favors for it! Now, Elgin wasn't a homosexual, but his hunger for dope proved to be too strong for him. So much so that he handed over his manhood on a silver platter for it. His conscience had been fucking with him ever since, but he was sure the dope would make him feel better about his decision shortly.

Elgin buckled his belt around his arm, which caused his veins to become pronounced. Finding one he had in mind, he spat on it and rubbed his saliva into it, leaving a shiny spot behind. A roach crawled out of his hair, down his forehead, and onto his cheek. He smacked it away, and it fell on the ground on its back, kicking its legs wildly before dying. Elgin picked up the syringe he'd already prepared and squirted some of its contents out of it. He licked his beige and decaying teeth thirstily and went to inject himself with the dope when a flicker of movement in the darkness caught his eyes. He leaned forward and narrowed his eyes into slits, trying to see who it was in his dilapidated house.

"Who is it? Who's there?" Elgin asked as he continued to try to peer through the darkness. Sweat ran down the side of his face, and his heart thudded. A lump of nervousness formed in his throat as he saw the flicker of movement again. Someone was coming forward, taking cool, calm, and collected steps.

Elgin didn't know who it was that had invaded his home. He'd done so much scandalous shit in his life that the list of people that wanted to see him dead was as long as the Great Wall of China. That couldn't have been anyone advancing in his direction from the other side of his shithole of a living room. Feeling the threat against his life lingering over his head like a dark cloud, Elgin knew he had to do something if he planned to live to get high another day. With that in mind, his head whipped from left to right, looking frantically for something to defend himself with. His eyes landed on an empty Corona bottle on the coffee table. Roaches were crawling all over it.

Swiftly, Elgin dropped the syringe and snatched up the Corona bottle. Holding it by its neck, he slammed the end of it against the ledge of the table. The lower half of it exploded and left it with jagged edges. Elgin sprang to his feet and held up the broken bottle, its jagged edges twinkling from the soft light of the street lamps shining through the window behind him.

"Look, man, I don't know who the fuck you are, but if you come any closer, I'm gonna carve your face up something nasty," Elgin said threateningly. His face was twisted with hostility, and he was clenching his jaws. He was putting up one hell of a tough-guy performance, but he wasn't really with the shits. He was terrified and seconds away from pissing on himself.

The approaching man emerged from out of the darkness and calmly pulled the hood from over his head. As soon as his identity was revealed, Elgin's eyes bucked and his mouth flung open. He swallowed the ball of terror in his throat and his lips quivered. He couldn't believe his eyes, which was why he was blinking and wiping them.

"I—I—I thought you were—were—" Elgin stuttered awfully, but he was cut off shortly.

"Shhhh," the man said, holding his finger to his lips. "I was locked up, but now I'm free—free as a bird," Hellraiser told him with a solemn face. The look in his eyes said that he wasn't there to play games.

For the first time, Elgin noticed the gun he held at his side in his gloved hand. The sight of it made his heart thud harder than before. At that moment, he was terrified, but he was even more so terrified when he saw three more men emerge from the shadows. There was Mack, Julian, and Lil' Saint. They were all wearing gloves and packing heat.

"What—what are you—you here for?" Elgin asked fearfully. He hoped Hellraiser and his crew were there to do anything and everything except kill him. He could live with an ass whipping. A black eye, a busted lip, and a few broken ribs could heal, but there wasn't any coming back from death. At that moment, a big ass gray rat scurried across the raggedy, patched, stained carpet, but neither man seemed to notice it.

Hearing squeaking at his foot, Hellraiser looked down and saw a brown rat snooping around it. His eyes darted up at Elgin and then back down at the rat. Grunting, he stomped down on the rat twice, hearing it squeal and its bones crushing as he mashed its lifeless body into the floor.

"My bad," Hellraiser said nonchalantly. "Was that one of your aunts or uncles? Brothers perhaps?" He glared at Elgin as he grinded his teeth, flexing the bones in his jaws. Instantly, Elgin knew what he was getting at. There wasn't any doubt in his mind that the ex-con was there to kill him on the account of him snitching on him and putting him behind bars. "Yeahhhh, shit's finally starting to click, huh? I thought it would." Elgin became teary eyed and started trembling. He looked around at all of the hardened men and knew he wouldn't be able to talk himself out of his situation. All he could hope for was that they'd be merciful in their handling of him. But something told him he wouldn't be so lucky.

"I've been putting in work for as long as I can remember. I'm not bragging, and it's nothing that I'm proud of, but I've taken at minimum sixteen niggaz off the shelf," Hellraiser informed him. "I've never been caught for any of those bodies. As a matter of fact, the only murder beef I got caught up with is the one with Caleb. Now, it was dark as fuck that night, so I know for a fact no one saw my face. So, that means someone put chu up to dropping a dime on me. What I wanna know is, who? Who had it out for me so fucking bad? And why didn't they just kill me?"

"I—I don't know why they haddit out for you so bad," Elgin told him honestly. "And I don't know why they—they didn't just kill you. But I can tell you who—who was behind it."

"I'm listening," Hellraiser replied.

Tranay Adams

Chapter Twelve

"My nigga, three funky ass dollars? Are you serious?" Kojak spat angrily from inside the hood covering his head. He was a caramel-skinned youth with a three-week-old fade and the beginnings of a scruffy beard. He had a scar below his left eye, and his hazel-brown eyes were sinister and unforgiving. "You know good and goddamn well this ain't enough to cop from me." He balled up the wrinkled dollar bills and threw them at Elgin. The ball of dollar bills deflected off his chest and landed at his sneakers. Elgin snatched up the ball of money and shoved it into his pocket.

"Awww, man, come on now, don't do me like that," Elgin whined and complained. He was a scrawny man with a perm in his hair that showed signs of new growth. He had beady red eyes, big, ashy, chapped lips, and scars and scabs running up and down his arms. "You can't hook me up, as much as I spend witchu?" He scratched the inside of his arm, reopening scabs and causing them to bleed all over again.

Kojak looked at Elgin with disgust. Not only did his scratching sicken him, but he smelled like a sack full of sweaty assholes!

"Bruh, when was the last time you washed your ass?" Kojak frowned, pinched his nose closed, and took a step back from Elgin. "You fucking stink, back yo' ass up, nigga!" He motioned for Elgin to back away from him, and he did.

"I don't know, man, it's beena while," Elgin admitted. He continued to scratch the scabs on his arm, caking blood and dead skin underneath his fingernails. Kojak frowned harder seeing this. It made him want to throw up. "Look, Kojak, I'm sick, man. I mean, I'm really fucking sick. My stomach and shit cramping, and I've been—Aaarrrrr!" Elgin doubled over, holding his stomach. He vomited on the sidewalk and stained Kojak's Air Force Ones with slimy pink food particles.

"What the fuck, man!" Kojak said with disgust, trying to shake the slimy food particles from his sneaker. "I just copped these shits and you got cho nasty ass dopefiend goo on 'em!"

"I'm sorry, G, but I'm ill. I'm ill as fuck," a teary eyed Elgin said, with small strings of slime hanging from his bottom lip and chin. Breathing heavily, he pulled a bandana from out of his right back pocket and wiped his mouth with it. "I need—I need some boy bad, man, just gemme halfa bag." He reached for Kojak, but he snatched his arm back.

Kojak's eyebrows slanted and his nose scrunched, looking down at Elgin. "Mothafucking, dopefiend, I'm not giving you shit! But I'ma tell you what chu finna do, you finna clean off my mothafucking kicks!"

"Alright, I got chu—I got chu," Elgin assured him. He went to clean off Kojak's sneaker with his bandana, but he moved back.

"Not with that dirty-ass shit. Nigga, use yo' tongue!"

"My tongue?" Elgin's face balled up, looking back and forth between Kojak and the vomit on his sneaker. "Man, I'm not finna lick that shit off. What chu take me for? I may be a dopefiend, but I'm stilla fucking human being."

Kojak's nose scrunched further, and he clenched his jaws. As he reached inside of his pocket, he scanned the area for any potential witnesses. He didn't see any in sight, so he pulled out a small, black, rectangle-shaped box. He pressed a button on it and a four-inch blade sprang forth. It gleamed underneath the street lamp.

Kojak grabbed a fistful of Elgin's hair and yanked his head back, drawing a pained howl from him. "Check this out, homie, you gon' get down there and lick my Forces clean, or I'ma show you what your insides look like. You got that?" Kojak asked, clenching his teeth so hard his jaws pulsated. He clutched Elgin's hair tighter, and his face wrinkled painfully.

"I got it, bruh! I got it!" Elgin assured him, wincing. When Kojak released him, he fell back down on all fours. Kojak placed his stained sneaker before him, and he reluctantly brought his face downward, sticking out his wet tongue. Kojak smiled wickedly, seeing Elgin's tongue about to grace the toe of his sneaker. Suddenly, Elgin came up and punched Kojak in his balls as hard as he could!

134

"Ooof!" Kojak groaned in pain, crossing his eyes, with veins bulging on his neck and forehead. Instantly, he dropped his knife and grabbed between his legs, falling to his knees. He was in so much pain, his eyes overflowed with tears and spilled down his cheeks.

"I'ma human being, goddamn it! A human being!" Elgin said over and over again as he got to his scuffed-up high-top sneakers. The laces in them were so dirty they looked black, and the sneakers themselves were so filthy they looked more gray than white. Once he was standing upright, Elgin kicked Kojak across his chin. The dope boy fell to the sidewalk dazed, confused, and bleeding at his mouth.

Elgin farted and threw up a little more before he kneeled down to Kojak. He rifled through both of his pockets, spilling loose change, dollar bills, and two packages of dope. He smiled broadly and put his yellowing, plaque-stained teeth on display.

"I'ma kill you—I'ma putta bullet right between your fucking eyes!" Kojak promised, wincing in agony and holding himself. He attempted to get up. Elgin kicked him in his side, tossing him over on his back. He then took off down the sidewalk as fast as he could, farting and holding the ass of his tattered jeans. His lack of dope left him nauseated and with the bubble guts. He had to shit, and he had to shit bad! But most importantly, he had to get his dose of medication. His insides were wreaking havoc on him, and he didn't know how much more he could take.

"This isn't the last you'll hear from me, you mothafucking junkie! You hear me you, cocksuckaaaaa!" Kojak screamed at the top of his lungs as he lay on his side, looking at Elgin zig zag across the street, avoiding getting hit by cars, zipping back and forth. The speeding vehicles honked their horns and hurled insults at Elgin.

"Watch where you're going, asshole!" a middle-aged white man hollered from his Bronco, wagging his fist at Elgin threateningly.

Boomp!

A black Chevy Caprice Classic collided with Elgin, and he went rolling up its windshield. He rolled back off the Chevrolet and smacked down upon the pavement. The Chevy stopped and the driver's door swung open. A pair of navy-blue Nike Cortez touched the asphalt one at a time. Horns sounded off all around the driver as he made his way toward Elgin.

"Uhhhhh!" Elgin groaned in pain as he picked his face up from the ground. He looked around, wincing and feeling the aches in his back. He scanned the surrounding grounds for his packages of dope. When he spotted them, they were lying in front of the driver who was rocking the Nike Cortez'. The driver, who went by the name Forty because he was twenty years old and looked twice that age, mashed out the drugs into the pavement. Seeing his precious heroin being mashed out and scattered throughout the asphalt made Elgin want to cry. His bottom lip trembled, and his heart sank like he'd caught his high school sweetheart getting a train ran on her.

"You wanna steal from mothafuckaz, huh? Well, I got something for yo' ass!" Forty assured him as he reached inside of his bomber jacket with the tan fur around its hood. Elgin looked up at the young man, but he couldn't see his face. It was like the street lamps lit him just barely enough for anyone to see his mouth. Elgin could tell that it was definitely Kojak's right-hand man, Forty, though. His missing front tooth gave him away. Well, his missing tooth and the sound of his voice.

"Blast his ass, Forty, blast his ass!" Kojak called out from across the street, where he was slowly getting up on his feet, holding his aching balls and picking up his knife.

Elgin looked from Kojak to his main man, Forty. His eyes exploded open when he saw him pull out a .380 pistol and extend it in his direction.

"No, wait, please—" Elgin said shakily, squeezing his eyes shut and lifting his hands in surrender.

"Aaaaaaah!" Forty screamed as he was blinded by the head-lights of an oncoming vehicle. An old Ford Bronco slammed him

into the grill of his whip, making his hand swing aside and fire his pistol.

"Nooooooo!" Kojak screamed in the distance, having seen the Bronco collide with Forty. Gun in hand, he limped toward Elgin with every intention of killing him.

Elgin peeled his eyes open. He was surprised to see Forty impaled against the front of his car, staring at him accusingly, mouth hanging wide open. When Elgin looked in Kojak's direction, he found him coming after him, ringing out shot after shot. The sound of bullets pinging off metal and shattering the glass windows of the vehicles Forty was wedged between resonated through the air.

Elgin scrambled to his feet in a hurry and took off running down a nearby alley. His adrenaline was pumping crazily and his heart was raging. He could hear its rapid beating in his ears as he huffed and puffed, making hurried footsteps.

"Haa, haa, haa, haa, haa!" Elgin breathed heavily, looking back and forth over his shoulder. His face and body were so sweaty that he looked like he'd taken a bath in baby oil. In fact, he was so sweaty that his dirty wife beater was clinging to his frame. "Oh, shit, oh shit, oh shit!" he said over and over again, seeing Kojak's dark figure at the opposite end of the alley.

He was chasing after him, taking the occasional shot at him.

Blowl, blowl, blowl!

Elgin ducked and ran faster, hearing the bullets whizzing around him, coming deathly close to his head. His heroin hunger pains were at the back of his mind, and he was in survival mode now. Elgin took an awkward step and fell to the trashy ground. Picking himself right back up, he shook off his dizzy spell and kept on running.

Blowl, blowl, blowl, blowl!

Kojak kept busting at him, trying to take him off his feet. Sweat rolled down Elgin's forehead and seeped into his eye, burning it. Still running, he took the time to wipe his sweaty forehead and glance over his shoulder. When he looked, he saw two police cars swoop in behind Kojak, flashing their red and blue lights on him. The police jumped out of their whips and drew their guns, but unfortunately, Kojak already had the drop on them. He popped one in the jugular, and blood poured out of his neck. The cop dropped his gun and smacked his hand over the wound below his chin. Kojak popped another one of the pigs in the shoulder and a third one in the chest, slumping him against his vehicle. He went to lie down a forth pig, but before he could, the remaining ones opened fire on him.

Bloom, bloom, bloom! Blac, blac, blac, blac! Bloc, bloc, bloc, bloc!

Sparks and flames erupted from the hollow ends of One Time's guns chopping down Kojak where he stood. He fell to his death in a hail of bullets, blood, and gun smoke. By this time, Elgin had gotten halfway down the alley and had stopped running. He was hunched over with his hands on his knees and looking at what had transpired. Two of the pigs cautiously approached Kojak's body with their guns pointed at him. One of them kicked his foot twice to see if he'd respond, but he didn't. The other cop kicked his gun out of his reach and kneeled down to him, checking his pulse. He then looked to his partner, shook his head, and pretended to cut his throat. This was his way of letting him know that the young man was dead.

The cop that had gotten the word that Kojak had expired checked on the wounded officers and radioed in an ambulance to tend to them.

"Stupid son of a bitch." The cop that had kicked Kojak's foot looked at him and shook his head in pity. "He musta been high off something for 'em to try to shoot it out with us."

"Nah, someone had really pissed 'em off," the cop that had taken Kojak's pulse announced, standing back up on his feet. "He was definitely shooting at some…" The cop's words trailed off as he exchanged glances with his comrade. At the exact same time, they looked down the alley and found Elgin. His eyes exploded open, and his mouth dropped.

"Fuck," Elgin said loud enough for only him to hear.

"Aye, you, come here!" one of the cops called after Elgin.

138

"Oh, shit!" Elgin said, spooked, and took off running again. Up ahead, he saw a motorcyclist wearing a black helmet and matching black leather motorcycle jumpsuit. He was on a Kawasaki Ninja and making a U-turn in the middle of the street, narrowly missing a passing car. To his surprise, the motorcyclist swept up into the end of the alley, placed his boot to the ground to balance his bike, and motioned him over with his black leather-gloved hand. Elgin didn't know who the fuck the nigga was, but he was definitely glad he was willing to lend a helping hand.

I guess there issa God after all, Elgin thought as he ran up the alley, listening to the sounds of police car sirens at his back. He could hear a couple of them racing up behind him, with their red and blue lights flashing, lighting up the alleyway. He didn't bother looking over his shoulder, because he knew they were on his ass.

As soon as he hopped onto the back of the motorcyclist's Kawasaki Ninja, he hugged him around his waist, and he zipped off on the bike. He was going so fast that Elgin had to squint his eyes against the wind. The impact of the air was ruffling his long, unkempt hair as well as his wife beater. The motorcyclist glanced in his side-view mirror and saw two police cars spilling out of the alley, heading in his direction, but their presence didn't seem to faze him.

"They're on our ass, bruh! They're on our ass!" Elgin panicked after glancing behind him and seeing the police cars chasing after them. Right then, a police helicopter stole his attention as its propeller chopped through the air. As soon as Elgin glanced up, the helicopter shined its spotlight on them. The bright light caused him to place a hand above his eyebrows and narrow his eyes into slits. "A helicopter! A goddamn police helicopter is on us, bruh! Once one of them bitchez are on you, there ain't no escaping it!"

Right then, the silent motorcyclist revved up his Kawasaki Ninja and zipped up the street. His bike whined loud and disturbingly as it covered block after block with the helicopter following not too far behind. The motorcyclist popped a wheelie, leaving the back end of his motorcycle on the asphalt, as he zipped away from the spotlight of the helicopter. Elgin's face balled up and he held the motorcyclist tighter. The motorcyclist was going too fast for him. The level of speed he was going was making him nauseous, and he felt like he was going to throw up again.

Zooooooooom!

Loose trash and debris went up in the air as the motorcyclist whipped past an intersection, narrowly missing oncoming cars, whose drivers blew their horns frantically. The motorcyclist dipped in and out of traffic between vehicles coming and going, narrowly escaping clipping them. He hit a couple of sharp turns and almost hit a few pedestrians before he reached his destination: an underground shopping mall complex.

A few minutes later, several police cars with their sirens blaring entered the complex behind them, but they'd lost sight of them. The only thing left of the motorcyclist and Elgin's presence was the Kawasaki Ninja. It was parked perfectly in a parking space alone.

Meanwhile, the motorcyclist and Elgin made their way down a staircase as fast as they could. The motorcyclist was quick on his feet, but Elgin was huffing and puffing out of breath. He was having trouble keeping up, so the motorcyclist had to keep coming back for him. When they'd reached the landing to a door with a lit "exit" sign above it, the motorcyclist kicked it open and they spilled out into an alley. The motorcyclist looked up and down the alley. Spotting a white van with Hector's Carpet Cleaning Service on its back doors, he nudged Elgin and they ran toward it. The back doors of the van opened and a medium-built dude wearing a navy-blue cap and matching jumpsuit jumped down. He motioned the motorcyclist and Elgin forward while holding one of the doors open. The motorcyclist and Elgin jumped into the back of van. The nigga in the jumpsuit hopped in behind them and slammed the door shut. Right after, the van drove down the alleyway. The van had just made a left out of the alley when the door to the stairwell flew open. A second later, several armed cops spilled out, waving their guns and looking around for the motorcyclist and Elgin. Seeing the men weren't anywhere in sight, they lowered their guns. *Frustrated that the suspects had gotten away, one of the cops kicked a nearby trash bin and swung on the air.*

***

The Hector's Carpet Cleaning van pulled inside of a warehouse and stopped before an iron chair and a table. The vehicle was left idling as JayDee and Hot Boy hopped out of it. They were dressed in caps and navy-blue Dickie jumpsuits with the company's logo stitched on the back of them. Together, they pulled Elgin out of the van and drug him towards the iron chair. Their faces were scrunched up from the foul odor coming from Elgin. JayDee and Hot Boy's cheeks swelled and deflated like they were on the verge of throwing up. So, they held their breath as they drug him over to the iron chair.

"This mothafucking fiend stank something serious, bruh!" a frowning JayDee complained.

"You ain't never lied. If it wasn't for his breathing, I would have sworn ol' boy was dead," Hot Boy replied. He was frowning while holding his nose away from Elgin. If he breathed his stench any longer, he was sure he'd barf up the cherry slurpy and 7-11 hot dog he'd scarfed down earlier.

Elgin's wife beater was stained with crusting vomit, and the inside of his jeans was plastered with dry feces. His nose was runny and vomit had dried around his mouth. He'd been shitting and puking since he hadn't had any dope. He had one hell of a headache, and his stomach felt like Mike Tyson had been using it for a speed bag.

JayDee and Hot Boy planted Elgin in the iron chair. JayDee turned his cap backwards and grabbed the roll of duct tape from off the table. He went about the task of taping the dopefiend's arms and torso around the chair as well as his ankles. While he was doing this, Hot Boy closed the shutter of the warehouse and jogged back over to him and their hostage. Hearing the motorcyclist step down from the back of the van, JayDee and Hot Boy pulled out their guns. They stepped back and left a clear path to Elgin. The junkie's face was sweaty and he was breathing huskily. The nigga looked half-dead strapped to the chair. And to be honest, he probably was, especially if he didn't get some dope into his system.

The motorcyclist made his way towards Elgin, pulling off his helmet along the way. Elgin couldn't see his face on account of the darkness surrounding him, but he was nearing the lighting provided by the headlights of the van. The motorcyclist tossed his helmet upon the table and shook his locs loose, combing his gloves fingers through them. When he was finally standing before Elgin, he got a good look at him. He didn't know him personally, but he'd seen him around the hood often. He was a street nigga who wasn't a stranger to murder. In fact, he was well acquainted with it. It was his modus operandi!

"You don't know me, but allow me to introduce myself," the motorcyclist began. "I go by the name Hitt-Man, but my goons here call me boss man or boss dog. I know you're wondering why I saved your ass and brought you here. Well, I'll tell you, I need you to do a favor for me..." Hitt-Man told him he wanted him to report to the police that he'd witnessed a murder at a specific location. He wanted him to tell him that he saw Treymaine James kill Caleb. He picked up a manila envelope from the table and pulled out two photographs. He held the pictures up so Elgin could see them, telling him exactly who the two men were. Afterward, he tossed the photos onto the table and pulled a small packet of heroin with 'Killuh' stamped on it. Pinching it between his finger and thumb, he held it up so that Elgin could see. Instantly, the dopefiend perked up, and his eyes lit up seeing the object that was the key to ending his suffering. A smile spread across Hitt-Man's lips when he saw he'd gotten his hostage's interest. "You agree to do this favor for me and this baby is all yours right here and right now. Once you've completed the task, I've got nine more bags of this shit. And lemme tell you," with the packet of dope still pinched between his fingers, Hitt-Man leaned closer to Elgin and said in a hushed tone, "this shit will take you for a ride you'll never wanna get off of. So, what do ya say, my nigga? Are you up for the task or what?"

"Yeah, yeah, yeah, I'm with it," Elgin said fast, nodding. "Wherever you want me to go and whatever you need me to say, I will. Just—just release me from these bondages so I can shoot up."

"Aht, aht, aht," Hitt-Man said, shaking his finger from side to side. "It's notta deal 'til we shake onnit." He switched hands with the packet and extended his hand toward him. Elgin gave him the firmest handshake he could muster. With that, Hitt-Man gave the order for Hot Boy to cut Elgin loose. He then gave JayDee the order to bring the items to Elgin that he'd need to shoot up the heroin.

Once JayDee had everything on a metal tray, he took the packet from Hitt-Man and brought everything over to Elgin. He pulled the duct tape from his body and his ankles. He then licked his lips and rubbed his hands together in anticipation of feeling the drug coursing through his veins. As a matter of fact, his arms came alive with a tingling sensation. It was like they were excited to mingle with the poison inside of the packet as much as he was.

While Elgin was high, Hitt-Man had JayDee and Hot Boy see to it he got a haircut, a shower, and a fresh change of clothes. They wanted him to look like your average citizen when he went to report 'the murder he'd witnessed.'

Once Elgin had gotten cleaned up, JayDee and Hot Boy dropped him off at the corner across the street from the police station. He filed the false report, left the station, and got his other nine bags of dope as promised.

***

"Mothafucking Hitt-Man," Mack said angrily and balled his fists.

"I knew it was something up with that bitch-ass nigga," Julian said, clenching and unclenching his jaws.

"I'm not surprised. Not surprised at all," Lil' Saint stated of Hitt-Man's involvement in putting Hellraiser behind bars.

The news didn't move Hellraiser at all. He didn't put anything past anyone, especially a nigga like Hitt-Man. His main objective now was to find him and turn his lights out. But right before he put him to sleep, he wanted him to tell him what was his reasoning behind doing what he'd done to him. Afterwards, he'd make Assassin pay for what he'd done to KiMani and Arnez.

This shit deeper than what I think. Hitt-Man could have easily just clapped me, but he decided to get me caged up instead. Fuck it! I'll find out when it comes down to it, Hellraiser thought, and then focused his attention on Elgin. The look he gave the dope-fiend made him uneasy. He felt like he was going to shit on himself. In fact, the mothafucka farted, filling the room with an unbearable stench that caused the rest of the crew to frown and turn their heads.

"Thanks for that bit of info," Hellraiser told Elgin. "But unfortunately, your time has passed. You ready to die, nigga?"

Elgin's heart skipped a beat when he was asked this. His stomach twisted in knots, and he thought he was going to throw up. He was sure he was going to die now. There was no way he could talk his way out of this situation. With that in mind, Elgin decided to die with some dignity. His face twisted into a mask of hatred. He released a battle cry, charging full speed ahead at Hellraiser, ready to slash his throat with the jagged edges of the bottle.

"Aaaahhh!" Elgin screamed and held the broken bottle up. He was closing the distance between him and Hellraiser quickly. He'd gotten halfway across the living room when all of the OGs upped their guns and blew his ass down!

Muzzle flashes from the OGs' blowers lit up the living room. It sounded like thirty firecrackers going off. Once they lowered their guns from firing, Elgin collapsed to the floor. The smell of blood and gun smoke was heavy in the room. Seeing a bloody Elgin was still clinging to life, wheezing and squirming, Hellraiser reloaded his piece and walked over to him.

He found the dopefiend with tears pouring out the corners of his eyes and coughing up blood. He was filled with so many holes he looked like he'd gotten dressed up in all red that day.

Hellraiser took the time to admire his and his crew's handi-work before pointing his gun at Elgin's face. Elgin's eyes blinked repeatedly, and he started choking on his own plasma. He stared up at Hellraiser accusingly. Then they came back to back—the bullets that would end his life!

Bocka, bocka, bocka, bocka, bocka!

Hitt-Man was the only nigga that knew I was there to kill Caleb. That means he set me up to kill him so I'd get locked up and he'd be free to take over his organization, Hellraiser thought as he lowered his smoking gun. *What I don't get is why he didn't just pop my ass so he wouldn't have to worry about me later? Whatever his reasons for allowing me to live, he's gonna regret it. That's on my momma's grave.*

Hellraiser watched as Elgin's thick blood poured out of his head and body, saturating the floor. After tossing the murder weapon beside his kill, he walked away with his crew following behind him.

The original gangstas had returned!

Tranay Adams

Chapter Thirteen

Whack!

An enraged Zekey swung an aluminum baseball bat against the fifty-inch television and cracked its screen into a cobweb. Sparks flew out of it and electricity surged through. He cocked the baseball bat around his shoulder and swung it with all his might. His eyebrows were slanted, his nose was scrunched, and his top lip was peeled back in a sneer. His eyes were pink and tears were streaming down his face. He'd just watched a Channel 5 Action News report about a shooting that left KiMani seriously injured and in a coma and Arnez dead.

Quan stood by silently crying and watching her husband take his frustrations out on the television set. She wanted to stop him but felt it was best to let him take his anger out on the TV.

Whack, whack, whack!

Zekey beat the flat-screen television until it fell from the wall and crashed to the floor. Spreading his legs, he cocked the baseball bat over his head and brought it down on the TV again and again. Quan had never seen him behave in such a manor, but she was glad Ali was at her mother's house. She didn't want him seeing his stepfather out of his mind and out of control.

Whack, whack, whack, whack!

Zekey battered the television until he was tired and sweaty. Still holding the baseball bat, he dropped down to his knees and bowed his head. Holding his hand over his face, he broke down sobbing. Tears flooded his cheeks and his shoulders rocked back and forth. Quan wasn't sure what she should do since she'd never been in this situation with him before. Swallowing her spit, she took a deep breath, and reluctantly walked over to her man. Hesitantly, she placed her hand on his shoulder and then got down on her knees. She hugged him and allowed him to cry in her arms. He dropped the baseball bat and held onto her. She cried as he cried, hating to see him in such a state. She knew how much Arnez meant to him. The tattoo of the young nigga's face on his left peck and his talking about him made that evident.

"It's going to be all right, baby. We're going to get through this," Quan said, kissing the side of his head and rubbing his back.

Zekey was overwhelmed with hurt and guilt. Arnez being murdered was partially his fault. If he hadn't given Hitt-Man's people KiMani's address, then Arnez would still be alive.

Zekey swore revenge on those that carried out Arnez's hit. He was going to see to it that all parties involved got the business behind his little homie. He was a rider for his, and Hitt-Man's goons were going to wish they'd never fucked him over.

Zekey stopped crying and wiped his eyes. He got up from the floor with the assistance of Quan and his baseball bat. When he stood upright, he was staring at his reflection in the rectangle-shaped mirror hanging over the couch. He had bags under his eyes and his cheeks were wet from crying. Pulling away from Quan, he approached the mirror while yanking open his shirt and sending buttons flying. He felt on the tattoo of Arnez he'd gotten on his chest. His touching it brought on the wonderful memories they'd shared together.

"I'ma make 'em pay me in blood—all of 'em!" Zekey shouted heatedly. "On everything I love, nephew, I'm at these bitch-ass niggaz' necks like Dracula!"

"That's right, daddy. And I'ma be there to back you up," Quan assured him. She walked up behind him, wrapping her arms around his waist and kissing him on the back of his head. "Ali and I loved Arnez too. He was a part of our family," she told him. "Blood will answer for blood."

"That's why I love you so much, lil' mama, you always got my back," Zekey said, turning around to face her.

"And always will, daddy. I'm your ride or die," Quan replied. She was saying this while looking up at him lovingly.

"Them niggaz that laid down nephew are gonna get theirs, no doubt," he assured her. "But in the meantime, I'm riding on the young boy, KiMani."

"KiMani?" She frowned, trying to recall the name. She was sure she'd heard it before.

"Yeah, mamas, KiMani," he told her. "The pup that got me wearing this shit for the rest of my life." He pointed to the hearing aid in his ear.

"However you wanna play it, daddy. Just know I got chu," Quan said as he brushed her braids out of her face and looked her in her eyes. He admired her beauty openly.

"I'll fill you in on my plan while we take a shower. Come on." Zekey took her hand, tossed the baseball bat aside, and led her towards the bathroom.

Thanks to the news report, Zekey knew what hospital KiMani was in, so all he had to do was find out his room number. It just so happened the facility he was being treated at was the same one that Quan worked at as a nurse's assistant. Now, Zekey knew he couldn't get up there as himself, so he planned on duplicating her employee's badge with a picture of himself. He'd be going up there disguised as a white female nurse. He was confident he'd slip by the hospital's staff undetected to kill KiMani once and for all.

***

Two nurses in scrubs made their way out of the back exit door of the hospital, talking among each other. One of them was white with blonde hair and blue eyes while the other was a sister with micro individual braids she wore in a bun. They were so engrossed in their conversation that they didn't notice Zekey laid in the cut. He was wearing hazel-green contacts, a brunette wig, and makeup that made him look like an older Caucasian woman. His attire was powder blue scrubs and old white sneakers with scuff marks on them.

Zekey, who was still hidden in the shadows, looped the string of an identification badge over his head, which he'd taken the time to craft himself. Hunched down on his knees, he made hurried footsteps towards the exit door, which was quickly closing. He managed to slip through the opening of the door right before it closed. Once he was inside, he sighed with relief and wiped away the sweat on his forehead. Then he proceeded across the floor where he checked in with the guard at the front desk. He'd already called the hospital to see exactly what room KiMani was in, so he didn't have to worry about finding out now that he was there.

Once Zekey had signed in at the guard's desk, he made his way down the hallway towards the elevator lobby. He hopped on the elevator and hopped off on the floor he'd requested. He greeted and waved to the hospital staff he crossed paths with in the corridor.

Blood, this shitta 'bouta be a piece of cake. These crackaz don't even know it's a straight-up killa behind this guise, Zekey thought as he walked down the hallway, looking at the numbers of the rooms on either side of him. He smiled satanically when he spotted the hospital room KiMani was assigned. His revenge was only a few steps away, and he could feel his dick getting hard in anticipation of it.

"What the fuck?" Zekey's eyes bulged and stopped in his tracks. He saw Arnez standing at the end of the corridor, shaking his head with disappointment. He squeezed his eyes shut and then popped them back open. Arnez had vanished! He looked up and down the corridor for him, but he didn't see him. Figuring his mind was playing tricks on him, he massaged between his eyes. He turned inside the room KiMani was housed and met darkness. In fact, the only light was the soft ones coming from the screens of the medical machinery.

Zekey looked to the other side of the room. His brows wrinkled when he saw Lachaun and Billion lying asleep in the neighboring bed. He didn't see them as a threat, but if they proved to be one, he'd snuck in a weapon. Since he couldn't get a gun past the metal detectors, he'd improvised and brought along a dagger he'd made out of Plexiglas.

"You know, kid, I'ma man of honor and respect," Zekey spoke to KiMani as he entered his room. "I don't find it honorable to kill a man who can't defend himself, but in your case, I'm willing to make an exception. I've been dreaming about whacking yo' lil' young ass for the past five years, and finally, here's my chance. I'd be a damn fool notta take it." While he was giving this speech, he was clicking off all the medical machinery. He knew once he performed what he deemed a necessary evil, the machines would go wild, alerting the hospital staff to KiMani's spiritual departure. "Although I'd rather make this entire ordeal long, painful, and bloody, outta respect for nephew, I'ma make this clean and as quick as possible. So, consider yourself lucky," Zekey said this while his hand traveled up the length of the clear tube attached to KiMani's oxygen face mask.

He took the tube into his hand and bent it with his thumb, cutting off the oxygen flowing to KiMani's lungs. After a full minute, the fingers of KiMani's left hand began to twitch. First, it was his pinky finger, then the finger next to it. The fingers of his other hand began to twitch too. Next, his eyelids and nose began twitching as well.

Zekey smiled satanically again, seeing the young man strug- gling to breathe. Still holding the tube closed, he took the time to glance at his watch. KiMani had gone a minute and a half without oxygen. While Zekey was locked up on his robbery charge, he did a lot of reading, especially about the human anatomy. He learned the ins and outs of the body's functions and found them remarka- ble. For instance, the human body couldn't go any longer than three to six minutes without oxygen. Any longer than that, and you ran the risk of irreversible brain damage, or even worse—death.

"Three more minutes and it's bye, bye," Zekey said, waving goodbye to KiMani. When he looked up, he saw Arnez standing on the opposite side of the bed. Again, he was shaking his head in disappointment, like he wasn't feeling what he was doing. Zekey was shocked at first but figured he was tripping again. So, he squeezed his eyes shut and popped them open. Again, Arnez had vanished, but he could still feel his presence nearby.

"Unc, stop," Arnez said from behind him. Zekey felt a hand on his shoulder and whipped around. He didn't see anyone behind him.

"Nephew? I thought you were dead," Zekey asked, eyes scanning the room. "Where are you?"

"Right here," Arnez replied. Zekey looked to his left and he wasn't there. "Not there, here."

Zekey looked ahead, and Arnez was standing on the opposite side of KiMani's bed again. His face was hidden in the shadows, and he could only make him out from the chest down.

"You're—you're still alive?" Zekey asked with wrinkled brows.

"Nah," Arnez replied. "I've come to stop you from killing my brotha. I love this nigga right here to death." He looked to KiMani and grasped his hand affectionately. "I'd like you to dead the beef, and let my nigga be, man. If you love me like you claim you do, please, leave 'em be—for me." He looked in Zekey's direction, but the older man still couldn't see his face, thanks to the shadows.

Zekey's vision became obscured with tears, and a teardrop fell from his right eye. He wiped his dripping eye with his curled finger and took a breath. He loved and missed Arnez and hated the fact that he was dead.

"Okay, nephew, okay." Zekey nodded and released the tube that led to the oxygen mask. "Shit is squashed. I'ma let youngin' live, but it's only 'cause of you." He pointed at him then wiped his wet face.

"Thank you," Arnez said and walked around the bed to him, opening his arms. Zekey hugged him and shut his eyes, tears jetting down his cheeks. "I love you, Unc. Always have and always will."

"I love you too, nephew," Zekey replied. His voice cracked emotionally.

Zekey's eyes popped open, and he found his arms empty. He scanned the room for Arnez's whereabouts, but he'd vanished—like a ghost. Zekey sniffled, took the time to wipe his face, and gathered his wits. He then leaned closer to KiMani's ear. He'd heard through word of mouth that people in a coma could still hear you when you talked to them.

"On the strength of Arnez, the beef I got witchu is dead," Zekey informed him. "You don't have to worry about me coming at cho head no more—that's my word. From now on, in honor of

Arnez, I'm on them fools' asses that got at him and you." He then pulled the blanket further up on KiMani and turned on all of the medical machinery he'd turned off upon entering.

Zekey took one last look at KiMani before leaving his room. As he traveled down the hallway, thoughts of murdering Arnez's killaz went through his mind.

Niggaz abouta feel my pain, Zekey thought as tears slid down his cheeks and he balled his fists. He hurried downstairs where Quan was waiting for him next door in a Shell gas station. As soon as he hopped into the passenger seat, he slammed the door shut and snatched off his wig. He was in the middle of popping out his hazel contact lenses when Quan was driving away.

***

Hitt-Man was behind the wheel of his blood-red 2015 Bentley Bentayga truck. He drove through the scarce streets with a sexy little number in his passenger seat. She had a chocolate complexion and wore her hair in a short style. She had mesmerizing brown eyes, remarkable lips, big perky breasts, and hips that wouldn't quit. The woman's name was Valencia. She was the younger, prettier version of Niqua and the latest reason behind her insecurities, and rightfully so. Hitt-Man couldn't keep his hands off this bitch.

Hitt-Man had promised Niqua long ago he'd never fuck a broad behind her back. They made an agreement to only have threesomes together, so technically, this nigga was cheating. He'd told Niqua he was going out for a night on the town with the fellas. They were going to have a couple of drinks at Club Mack Daddy, trick off with some strippers, and probably hit up the craps table at Hollywood Casino.

Hitt-Man's bullshit story sounded so good he convinced himself he was telling the truth. What he'd really gone to do was pick up Valencia from her crib. They went out for dinner and a movie, and now they were headed to the Ritz-Carlton to smash. Valencia had some bomb-ass pussy, and Hitt-Man was gone wear that ass out as soon as they got into their suite. But right now, he was horny as shit and needed to catch a nut before they made it to the hotel. With that in mind, he figured getting his dick sucked would hold him over until they got to their destination.

Keeping one hand on the steering wheel, Hitt-Man unbuckled his belt and unzipped his jeans. He pulled his semi-hard meat out of its denim prison and guided Valencia's head toward it. She held his shit at its base and took it between her awaiting lips. Hitt-Man threw his head back, moaning upon feeling the texture of her wet tongue and the 98-degree temperature of her mouth. Her eyes rolled to the back of her head as she passionately sucked his piece, coating it with her warm saliva, and stroking it at the same time. Her feminine moans filled the interior of the luxury SUV and became music to his ears. Her sensual noises made his dick double in size, becoming harder. Now his mushroom tip was engorged and big, juicy veins were running up and down his shaft.

"Damn, ma, you got the best head in the world," Hitt-Man told her as he rolled his eyes and basked in the pleasure her mouth bestowed upon him.

"Mmmmmummmm," Valencia moaned and groaned, sucking his shit long and strong. Coat after coat of her saliva slid down his endowment and soiled his nut sack. She started sucking on the most sensitive area of his dick, which was the head, while continuously pumping it.

"Ahhh, fuck, blood!" Hitt-Man grunted and fought to keep his hooded eyes on the road. He found himself pushing up from off his seat and jabbing the inside of Valencia's mouth. Nasty sloshing and squishing noises accompanied by her gagging consumed the confines of the SUV. Hitt-Man's tongue hung out the corner of his mouth as he vigorously humped inside of her mouth. "Yeah, yeah, yeah, I'm 'bouta nut! I'm 'bouta nut deep down yo' mothafucking throat! Massage my balls, ma! Massage my shit!" His voice strained as he neared his climax. The feel of her touch, the gagging, and the spit sliding down his dick became too much for him and he was about to erupt, until—

Boom!

154

The force of something crashing into the Bentley truck caused Valencia to nick Hitt-Man's dick. The climax he felt coming on vanished and was replaced by a slight stinging pain. He grimaced and she swung her head back up. She frowned, wondering what the fuck had crashed into them as she wiped away the blood at the corner of her mouth. Valencia looked through the back window and was instantly blinded by the high-beam headlights of a vehicle she couldn't make out.

"Ah, shit, my shit bleeding!" Hitt-Man announced after glancing down at his shiny, bleeding dick. "Who the fuck was that? Can you see 'em?" He glanced in the rearview mirror and saw the bright headlights of the vehicle. Upon further inspection, he realized it was a van. "I don't know who they are, but they're about to slam into us again," Valencia said hysterically. Her heart quickened, and she began to panic. She knew Hitt-Man was involved in the streets, so this situation could very well be a hit squad sent to take him out.

"Okay, open the glove compartment and grab my shit outta there!" Hitt-Man told her. "It's already cocked and ready, you just gotta hand it to me."

"Okay." A trembling Valencia nodded and wiped away the wetness from her eyes. She popped open the glove box and found a nickel-plated Desert Eagle lying on top of the truck's registration and owner's manual. She snatched the Desert Eagle out and smacked the glove box closed. She went to pass the gun to Hitt-Man and—*Boom!*—the van crashed into them again. The impact knocked the Bentley off course, but Hitt-Man managed to recover it.

"Fuck! Gemme the gun, hurry up," Hitt-Man told Valencia then activated his Bluetooth. He called up another one of his trusted goons. The phone rang and rang!

"I dropped it!" Valencia cried, looking around on the floor for the Desert Eagle.

"You dropped it? What the fuck! Find it! Hurry! These niggaz are on our ass!" Hitt-Man told her, looking back and forth between the windshield and Valencia.

Valencia made a funny face as she felt under the passenger seat for the gun. A look of relief came over her face when her hand grazed the weapon's handle. "I've found it! I've got it!"

"Boss dog, what up?" Nate's voice came over the speakers of the truck.

"I need you, ASAP, youngin'. The opps are on my ass!" Hitt-Man replied, taking his Desert Eagle from Valencia.

"Say no more. I'm in the streets with a band of my niggaz now," Nate told him, seriousness dripping from his tone. "Just tell me where you a—"

Boom!

Nate was cut short by the van crashing into the back of the Bentley truck again. Hitt-Man dropped his Desert Eagle. He tried to regain control of the bulky luxury vehicle as it sped out of control, but his efforts were useless.

"Aaaahhhh! Aaaaahhhh! Aaaaahhhh!" Valencia screamed over and over again as the truck spun around. It eventually flipped and tumbled down the street. The SUV landed upside down at the corner of Normandie and Imperial Highway, right beside Southwest Community College.

The wrecked Bentley Bentayga truck was ignited by a small flame while it trickled gasoline from its busted tank. Hitt-Man and Valencia lay upside down on the ceiling of the truck. They had bloody gashes on their foreheads, and the broken pieces of glass littering their clothing twinkled. The windshield of the vehicle was shattered, and its broken pieces of glass lay sprawled on the ceiling. Hitt-Man and Valencia groaned and grimaced. They had splitting headaches and were sore all over.

Hitt-Man stared at the van as it quickly approached them. There was blood in his right eye, so he saw everything in that shade. Whoever had caused the crash was coming to finish them off, and he didn't plan on making the job easy for them. He turned himself around inside of the SUV and looked around for his Desert Eagle. He found it about seven feet away from the wreckage. He began his crawl through all of the broken glass out of the windshield. He sliced up his hands during the process but paid his wounds no mind. They would be the least of his problem if he couldn't manage to fight off whoever intended to kill him.

"Aaaah, aahh!" Hitt-Man grimaced as he pulled himself along. Barely conscious, Valencia watched him crawl past her, wondering where he was going. Her right arm was broken, and any movement of it brought her horrible aches and pains. Still, she was going to try her best to escape whatever pending doom was looming over both of their heads. With that thought in mind, she started kicking at the fractured passenger window to make her escape. The fracture in the window grew bigger and bigger until the glass gave.

Uuuuurrrrrk!

The Astro van came to a halt outside of the Bentley Bentayga, and two masked gunmen hopped out. They were wearing black fatigues and toting Tavor TAR-21 assault rifles. Valencia's eyes exploded open in fear, and her jaw dropped. She knew she was in grave danger and didn't stand a snowball's chance in hell against the masked gunmen, but she was still going to put up a fight.

Valencia grabbed her purse with her functioning hand and dumped out its contents. She rifled through the items with her hands until she came across the can of mace. She was about to grasp it when a powerful force snatched her out of the truck through the broken passenger window.

"Aaaaahhhh!" Valencia screamed as she was pulled across the pavement through broken glass. Looking over her shoulder, she saw one of the masked gunmen pulling on her. He stopped once he'd felt like he'd pulled her far enough from the wrecked Bentley. "Oh, God no, please, please don't kill me, please!"

The masked gunman reached down to grab her, and she turned around, kicking him in the face. He stumbled backward and grabbed his face. Valencia got up as fast as she could with her functioning hand. Once she was upright, she limped away as fast as she could from the gunman. Her head was on a swivel as she looked around for someone to help her. Her vision was obscured from the fresh tears that filled her eyes.

"Hellllp, hellllp, someone help me! Pleeaaase!" Valencia screamed over and over again, searching for somewhere to escape. Her eyes went across the other masked gunman who was going after Hitt-Man, but she wasn't worried about him. He'd have to find for himself. She had herself to worry about. "Hellllp, hellllp, hellllp me, please!" She limped toward the sidewalk and occasionally glanced over her shoulder. The masked gunman that had dragged her out of the truck was coming after her with his Tavor TAR-21 assault rifle held low. Her heart thudded mercilessly and she limped away faster.

Pop, pop, pop, pop, pop, pop!

Bullet after bullet zipped out of the barrel of the gunman's Tavor TAR-21 assault rifle and chopped Valencia down. Her limp body collided with the street. Her eyes and mouth were wide open. She was wearing the face of death!

Hitt-Man made it out of the shattered windshield and tried to get up on his feet. He made it up on one leg but winded up falling back down to the pavement. That's when he realized his left leg was broken and bloody. A bone shard was sticking out from his calf.

"Grrrrr, shit!" Hitt-Man growled lowly, like an angry lion. It was like as soon as he looked back at his leg, the pain that was non-existent came rushing to him all at once. It hurt like a son of a bitch, but his mind was quickly taken off of it, seeing one of the gunmen closing in on him. He focused his attention back on his Desert Eagle, crawling for it faster and faster. He was coming up on it fast. He'd nearly closed the distance between it and himself when shots rang out dangerously loud.

Pop, pop, pop, pop, pop!

Debris and broken pavement flew up into the air as the Desert Eagle was shot far from Hitt-Man's grasp. He looked like he'd been stabbed through the heart when the only way to defend himself was taken from him. He could hear the heavy booted footsteps of the masked gunman coming up behind him. He knew he was the one that had shot the gun out of his reach when he looked to the ground and saw his shadow coming up from behind him. The next thing he knew, he felt his boot mashing his wounded calf into the pavement, treating it like it was a discarded cigarette.

"Gaaah!" Hitt-Man hollered out, feeling the sensational pain spread up his leg. He made an ugly ass face as his calf ground into the street. Blood oozed out of his wound and soaked into the surface below. Once the masked gunman ground Hitt-Man's calf into the ground, he stomped it one last time for good measure, making him holler in agony. He then made his way around to the side of him, using his boot to push him over onto his back, and leveling his assault rifle at his face. "What, mothafucka, you expect me to beg for my life? Well, you got me fucked up, homeboy! I'ma original gangsta, an OG! Give it to me how I got it, nigga! What's up?"

"Shut the fuck up!" the masked gunman barked heatedly and shot off his left ear. Hitt-Man hollered so loud he felt like his eardrums were going to rupture. He gritted and clutched what was left of his ear, blood seeping between his fingers. He settled his angry eyes on the masked gunman. It was from the expression on his face that the masked gunman knew he'd kill him if given the chance.

"I want chu to take a good look at me, 'cause my face will be the last one you see before you die." The masked gunman took his gloved left hand from his assault rifle and pulled his ski mask above his brows. He smiled wickedly from ear to ear and bit down on his bottom lip. He nodded his head like, yeah, nigga, I caught that ass slipping.

Hitt-Man stared up at the gunman with disbelief. After all this time, he was sure he was dead, but he'd been sadly mistaken. He really didn't know what to say about the revelation revealed to him. He understood he was on the losing end of this situation, and he was ready to see if his final resting place would be Heaven or Hell.

"Fuck you waiting on, nigga? Satan ain't got all d—" Hitt-Man was cut short when a burst of gunfire blew what was inside of his head on the outside. His brain fragments looked like shrimp smothered in Ragu spaghetti sauce. He was definitely dead, but that didn't stop the masked gunman from emptying what was left in his clip into his chest. As the barrel of his machine gun smoked, he took the time to pull his ski mask back down over his face and reloaded it. The van he'd come in skirted to a halt behind him. He turned around and ran over to it, hopping into the side door of it, which was already open. As the van sped off, he pulled its side door closed.

The van was long gone from the murder scene when police sirens filled the air. Shortly, a police helicopter patrolled the area, shining its spotlight over the dead bodies of Hitt-Man and Valencia. A white, brown, spotted, raggedy dog with missing patches of hair wandered over to Hitt-Man and started licking up his blood.

***

After putting Elgin's bitch ass to sleep, Hellraiser and the OGs went their separate ways with promises to link up later. Hellraiser returned to the hospital to spend the remainder of the night with his family. He came out of the elevator, made a left, and walked down the corridor. His aura screamed 'leave me the fuck alone, I'm going through some shit.' The hospital staff picked up on this. They whispered among each other as he walked past them. They wondered what was bothering him and thought of consoling him. But the spaced-out look in his eyes and the vibe was like repellant to them.

Hellraiser walked into KiMani's room and saw Lachaun sitting up in bed. She yawned and stretched her arms above her head. Her forehead creased when she saw him enter the room. She hopped off the bed and approached him.

"Baby, where you been?" Lachaun asked with concern.

Hellraiser didn't respond. He stood as still as a shit-stained statue in Central Park, with pigeons sitting on its head and shoulders.

"Treymaine, what's the matter?" Lachaun rephrased her question as she advanced toward him. The room was dark, so she could only make out his silhouette. It wasn't until she was two feet away that she could see his red-webbed eyes and the tears descending his cheeks. She started to worry then.

Abruptly, Hellraiser hugged Lachaun and caught her off guard. He broke down sobbing as he held on to her. She didn't know what was going on with him, but she was sure she'd find out later. Right now, her husband wanted and needed to be comforted, so that's exactly what she was going to do to him.

"Shhhh. Shhhh," Lachaun shushed him as she hugged him. She kissed him on the cheek as she ran her hand up and down his back soothingly. "Everything is going to be okay, baby. I got chu. I got chu," she assured him, rocking him from side to side, continuously rubbing his back.

Hellraiser's tears were for the families of the men that had tried to kill KiMani. The thought of causing someone else's parents the same heartache as him and his wife brought him great sorrow. He was devastated and overwhelmed emotionally. Still, he wasn't going to let his sympathy for his opps' mothers and fathers get in the way of him avenging his son. As far as he was concerned, the assassins that came after Kimani were dead men!

Chapter Fourteen

Hitt-Man's heroin empire had him living in the lap of luxury. Any and everything he could think of buying, he could obtain with a simple phone call. He owned five vehicles. A Bentley Bentayga truck, a Jaguar F-TYPE, a Porsche Macan turbo, a Ferrari Portofino, and a 1985 Chevrolet Silverado, all of which he kept parked in the circular soft-gray bricked driveway of his exotic-looking white concrete mansion. The three-million-dollar home looked like something out of a movie. Hell, for that matter, it looked like a crib only an A-list movie star could afford to purchase.

The mansion sat on 30 acres of beautifully kept land. It had an enormous pool in the backyard, a basketball court, and a tennis court, but what really set it off was the life-size statue of Hitt-Man dressed like a gladiator. He was holding a sword at his side in one hand while the other was holding up the severed head of Medusa. This statue was currently being defaced by a sledgehammer-swinging couple. They seemed to be getting a kick out of destroying one of the kingpin's most prized possessions.

"Fuck you waiting on, nigga? Satan ain't got all—*Boom*!" he said, reenacting the moment he blew Hitt-Man's head off. "I blew his shit back before he could finish whatever the fuck he was about to say!" He wiped the sweat from his forehead, gripped the sledgehammer with both hands, and swung it at the statue of Hitt-Man. The lower jaw of the statue exploded upon impact of the hammer. Smoke and fragments of the statue flew in every direction. Some of it deflected off him and Niqua. He took two more swings at the statue until he'd destroyed its head completely. He then lowered his hammer and rested his hands on top of its handle. He breathed heavily as sweat slid down the side of his face.

"I wish I coulda been there to see his face in that moment," Niqua said as she took the proper stance and hoisted up the sledgehammer. Her eyes were zeroed in on the part of the statue she planned to attack. "What was his reaction right before you pushed his shit back?" She swung the sledgehammer with all her might, and *boom*! The left arm of the statue exploded upon impact, sending a cloud of smoke and fragments flying. The pieces of the statue deflected off her eyewear and torso.

"I'ma keep it funky witchu, lil' mama." He started up again. "Homie went out like a straight up G. He wasn't whining like no ho or nothing. To be honest, in that moment, I couldn't be any happier to be his son," Assassin said with all honesty and truth dripping from his eyes.

"I'm not shocked by the way yo' father went out at all," Niqua replied as she lowered her sledgehammer and rested her hands upon it. "As long as I've known that stubborn son of a bitch, he's always stood on G shit."

"For real, for real," Assassin agreed. He went back to destroying the statue of his old man with the sledgehammer. Niqua joined him shortly. The fragments of the statue flew everywhere, some of it gathered at their feet on the lawn.

"You were right. Destroying this statue has made me feel a lot better," Niqua told him. "Even more so than you telling me you blew my trifling ass husband away."

"See, I told you I was gon' hold you down." Assassin dropped the sledgehammer and pulled her to him. She smiled, released the sledgehammer, and wrapped her arms around his neck. "I'm your king, and you're my queen. I'ma always be about us." They stared into each other's eyes for a moment, and then kissed for what seemed like an eternity.

"You promise that you're never gonna want anyone other than me?" Niqua asked him. She studied his face before he answered, trying to see if he'd show any signs of being disingenuous.

"I promise, queen. You're my only want and need," Assassin swore to her, looking her right in her eyes, gently caressing her cheek. "I'm 'bout whatever you 'bout, ma."

Niqua smiled happily and they kissed again.

***

"Get down on your knees!" Niqua ordered Assassin, but he didn't budge. He stared at her defiantly. This infuriated her so much she smacked him across the forehead with her piece. He fell to the ground, bleeding from the side of his forehead. Wincing, he stood back up on his knees and stared up at her. His face was scrunched up and his nostrils were flaring. He was pissed, more so at his father than her. It was his bidding that she was doing. "You brought that on yo' self youngin', I don't repeat myself to anyone!" She then leveled her gun between Assassin's eyes. The young gangsta didn't show any signs of fear. The blood of a G coursed through his veins, so he'd undoubtedly die like one.

"You know, it's funny, granted the situation I'm in, I feel more sorry for you right now," Assassin told her. She narrowed her eyes at him, wondering why he felt that way. He read her expression. "'Cause you're in the same situation my mother was in with my pops. I know your situation like it's my—"

"Aww, fuck what this nigga talking about!" Hot Boy said, frustrated. He didn't want to hear anything Assassin had to say. He wanted him dead and buried so he could carry on with his night.

"Shut the fuck up, Hot! The king ain't here, so the queen's running this show," Niqua said to him, then focused her attention back on Assassin.

"Like I was saying, 'I know your situation like it was my own,'" Assassin continued on with what he had to say. "When you were a lil' younger and your body was justa lil' tighter, he couldn't keep his hands off you. He swept you off your feet, wined you, dined you, romanced you—treated you like you was the only woman that mattered in the whole wide world. Stop me if I'm lying," he told Niqua. She didn't interrupt his story, so he continued on. "As time went on, the affection he showed you slowly started to dwindle. He seemed to grow disinterested in you intimately. The sex between you was practically non-existent. In fact, for him, having sex with chu felt like a chore..." By this time, the tears slowly accumulated in Niqua's eyes and spilled down her cheeks. She wiped them away with her free hand, but more spilled

down her face. He'd touched on a sensitive subject for her. She didn't know how he knew what he knew, but he was telling her the absolute truth. "Still in love with 'em, you were willing to do anything you had to for 'em to want chu as much as he did before. So, when he brought up the idea of inviting other women in the bedroom, you agreed to it. Only he started paying more attention to the other woman, which made you feel even more insecure— ugly even. At times, you felt yourself not being able to live without his love and you contemplated suicide. Now, ask me how I know all of this?"

"Man, shoot this nigga before I do!" JayDee shouted, lifting up his assault rifle and aiming it at the back of Assassin's head.

"You'll do no such thing. I'm the one here in charge! I'm the one!" Niqua shot back heatedly. Her face was slicked wet, and snot had oozed out of her left nostril. "So, you lower your gun, you lower your blower, right goddamn now!" JayDee clenched his teeth as he kept his assault rifle trained on the back of Assassin's head. He tossed the thought of killing Assassin back and forth across his mind but begrudgingly decided to stand down. He lowered his assault rifle down at his side, mad dogging Niqua, chest heaving up and down.

"Ask me how I know?" Assassin said again. His eyes were now a glassy pink, and he was on the verge of crying.

Niqua snorted the snot back up her nose and took a deep breath. "How—how do you know what chu know?"

"'Cause that bastard had my mother feeling the exact same way," Assassin admitted. "After he took away the best years of her life, he threw her away like she was a piece of trash. She couldn't stand the idea of the man she loved more than she loved herself no longer wanting her no more, so she killed herself." Tears broke down his face as his nostrils flared. "That's why I hate that mothafucka! That's how I could steal from 'em, and give 'em my ass to kiss."

"You said all of that to say what?" Niqua asked.

"If you were to let me go, I swear on my mother's grave, I'll treat you how you should be treated," Assassin told her, meaning

every word he spoke. "We'll have a relationship that only fairytales are made of, and I promise you'll fall harder in love with me than you have with any man. So, what do you say, goddess? You wanna give us a shot or what?"

"I can't believe this, are you really gonna buy this bullshit he's tryna sell?" Hot Boy asked Niqua. He found it hard that she didn't see Assassin was running game on her.

"That's what I'm saying, bro! Niqua, pop this nigga, man!" JayDee demanded. "He's just telling you all that shit so he can save his own—"

Niqua cut JayDee's sentence short by putting a bullet in his brain. Swiftly, she turned her gun to her right and pulled the trigger. Hot Boy was in the middle of lifting his assault rifle to lay her down when she sent fire at him. His bloody brain fragments flew out the back of his head, and he hurled backward. Niqua moved like a highly trained assassin, swinging her gun here and there, pulling its trigger. Empty shell casings spat from her gun and fire ignited from its barrel. Bullet after bullet zipped out of her lethal weapon, blowing out the brains of the rest of the goons.

When Niqua looked around the basement at all of the goons scattered on the floor, they were laid out with their blood pooling beneath them. The hounds were barking at Niqua angrily. Although they were dogs, they still recognized her betrayal. Her cellphone started ringing. She looked at her jack and saw it was Hitt-Man hitting her up. She knew she had to answer quickly or he'd suspect something. With that in mind, she shot the dogs dead and took a deep breath. Once she'd gathered herself, she answered her cellular.

"Nah, baby, everything is fine," Niqua said. She spoke to her husband while keeping her eyes on Assassin. He'd risen to his feet and signaled for her to free the zip tie binding his wrists. "You know who tried to make a move, but we handled it. I'm finna come up now. I love you. Muah!" She disconnected the call and put her cellular up. She then walked up on Assassin, placed her gun underneath his chin, and tilted it upward. "I took what you said to me to heart. You were very convincing—just like your old man.

But lemme be the first to tell you, if you don't live up to everything you said, I'm gonna treat you like a female Praying Mantis *would..." Assassin looked at her like he didn't know what the fuck she was talking about. And he didn't. "Fuck you. Then take your head clean off," she swore with threatening eyes and intimidation dripping from her lips.*

"I gotchu, lil' mama, you don't have nothing to worry about over here," Assassin swore to her and turned to the side so she'd see his restrained wrists. "Now, can you cut these off me, please?" Niqua nodded, pulled out a small Swiss Army knife, and cut him free. He turned around to her, rubbing his aching wrists. "Thanks. Listen, I'ma need to use yo' jack so I can call some of my people to clean this mess up."

Niqua nodded understandingly and gave him her cellphone. Assassin had a photographic memory, so he didn't have any trouble recalling the number he had in mind. He hit up Abrafo, his most trusted head busta, and told him the deal in so many words. Before he'd gotten off the cellular, Abrafo confirmed that he was going to pick up Montez and they were going to dip to where he was located. Afterwards, Assassin passed Niqua back her cellphone, pulled her close, and kissed her sensually.

Assassin loved everything about Niqua. He'd been feeling her since before she became his father's wife. He loved older women. Some of this was due to the fact he longed for a motherly figure since his mother's suicide. And she was the perfect one. She was as fine as wine, with big titties, a big ass, and chocolate skin that was dripping with melanin. As far as he could see, she seemed to be loyal but had a problem devoting herself to fuck niggaz. He was going to change all of that though. He was fucking with shorty hard!

"Gone head and dip off with Pops 'fore his faggot ass comes down here," Assassin told her. "Me and my niggaz are already gon' have a hard enough time finding some place to bury all of these bodies. The last thing we need is adding another one to the lot we already have."

168

"Yes." Niqua nodded and went to walk away, but he pulled her back.

Assassin tilted her chin upward and looked into her eyes. "Yes, what?" he asked her, looking at her like she knew better than that.

"Yes, daddy," she replied submissively. He kissed her once again and admired her ass as she walked away. He shook his head and massaged his chin. Thoughts of all the positions he was going to have her ass in when he finally fucked her went through his mind.

"Good," Assassin told her. "I need you to keep playing the role of submissive wifey to his cocky ass until I'm able to knock his head off. I memorized yo' number, and I'll be in contact shortly. I'll text you and let chu know what's the next move."

"Alright, boo," she replied.

Niqua tossed aside the gun she'd used to body the goons and headed up the staircase. As soon as she had disappeared, Assassin went to work pulling all of the bodies to one side of the basement. He grunted and sweated as he pulled them, leaving trails of their blood on the floor. The basement was overwhelmed with a foul odor of shit, piss, and blood from the goons having one last bowel movement after death.

Hitt-Man was sitting in the front passenger seat with his cell-phone glued to his ear when Niqua appeared outside the driver's door of his whip. He unlocked the doors of the vehicle through the operation panel on the passenger side door. She hopped in behind the wheel, strapped on the safety belt, and fired the truck up. She glanced up at the rearview mirror before pulling out of the parking space.

"Yeah, wifey just got in the truck just now," Hitt-Man informed whoever he was talking on his cellphone with.

"Babe, who was that?"

"Valencia. She says she's 'bout whatever we're 'bout tonight," a smiling Hitt-Man told her as he gave her thigh a gentle squeeze. "How 'bout it, babe? You tryna flip her lil' freaky ass tonight?"

169

Assassin was right! This nigga doesn't want me anymore, Niqua thought, becoming teary eyed. I don't understand it though. I gave 'em everything. I betrayed my family for 'em, gave my body to other women, killed on his behalf, all to satisfy him. Hmmmph, whata fool I've been. No more though. No more.

Niqua blinked back her tears and mustered up the most convincing smile she could.

"You don't even have to ask, big daddy," Niqua told him, sliding her pierced tongue across her top row of teeth, and then grasping the bulge in his jeans. "I'm with it all. Dick and pussy, I especially have a taste for Valencia's fine ass tonight."

Hitt-Man smiled harder and said, "You heard it straight from the horse's mouth, so what's up? You sliding through?" Valencia answered him. "Smooth. I'll send a car to pick up." He disconnected the call and sat his cellular aside. "Babe, setting this thang up for tonight done made a nigga horny as fuck. You think you could pet 'em while you drive?" He was referring to her jacking him off.

"I got chu, daddy. Gone and pull 'em out for Momma." Niqua smiled. Hitt-Man did just that. She spat on her hand twice, which left small strings of her slimy saliva hanging from her bottom lip. Using the spit as lubrication, she brushed it on her husband's piece and began to slowly caress his shit. He threw his head back, closed his eyes, licked his lips, and enjoyed the feminine stroking his wife gave him.

Niqua glanced back and forth between the windshield and Hitt-Man as she pleasured him. Her eyebrows were sloped and her nose was wrinkled. She was hot at him. But remembering what Assassin had told her, she continued to pleasure him.

Yeah, nigga, enjoy it while it lasts, 'cause you're living in your final days. Niqua smiled devilishly, looking like Satan. She knew the death of her husband was going to give her a sense of joy and hurt. But eventually, her heartache would subside, especially now since she had a man by her side who was going to love her the proper way.

170

***

When Niqua pulled back from kissing Assassin, she saw the gates of the mansion open and a white Chevrolet Tahoe heading their way. Assassin's brows crinkled, wondering what she was looking at, and he turned around. The Chevy truck parked on the white cobblestone driveway, and the driver killed its engine. The doors of the vehicle popped open and two men hopped out. Abrafo and Montez slammed the doors of the SUV and started over in Assassin and Niqua's direction. The king and queen of heroin lifted their protective eyewear to the top of their heads and waited for the killaz to approach.

"I take it y'all came bearing good news," Assassin asked them and folded his arms across his chest.

"Yeah, both those lil' niggaz dead," Montez replied.

"Both of 'em? You sure about that?" Niqua inquired.

"Hell yeah," Montez said. "I was raised as a shooter, that shit is my m.o."

Assassin nodded understandingly. Montez did have a reputation for busting his gun. His accuracy behind the trigger was second to none, which was why he'd recruited him. "You willing to bet your life on that, my nigga?"

Montez's brows wrinkled as he stared at Assassin. He glanced back at Abrafo to see what he had to say, but he didn't utter a word. So he looked back at Assassin and nodded assuredly.

"Yeah, I'm willing to bet my life onnit. I stand behind my work," Montez replied confidently. "Look, I've been holding this piss since before we left to earth them lil' niggaz, I'm finna go use y'all bathroom." He patted Assassin on his shoulder and made his way toward the mansion, stepping over the debris on the statue.

Once Montez was out of sight, Assassin focused his attention on Abrafo. "Did Tez blow dem boyz down like he said he did?" Abrafo nodded. "You vouch for 'em being dead?" The silent hitta gave him a look that he read fluently. "Right. Well, if he didn't carry out my orders to the fullest, you know what to do with 'em, right?" Abrafo gave him another look that he read into. The

African head hunter then stepped over the pieces of statue littering the lawn and headed toward the mansion.

"Alright, baby, let's get back to work," Assassin told Niqua as he took hold of his sledgehammer. The couple pulled their protective eyewear back down over their eyes, kissed, and went back to hammering away at what was left of Hitt-Man's statue.

Assassin knew all too well how easily it was to manipulate Niqua from watching his father's handling of her. She not only came from a broken home, but she suffered greatly from anxiety and depression. She desperately wanted to be loved and made to feel special by the opposite sex. Assassin took full advantage of this. He planned to use her just like his father had, and once he was done with her, he'd throw her away.

Assassin was going to play the role of the kind, caring, loving, and affectionate significant other to lower her guards. Then, once he knew without a doubt he was in her good graces, he was going to finesse the plug from her and take what his father built to another level.

Enjoy our time together while it lasts, sweetheart, 'cause it'll be coming to an end shortly, Assassin thought as he continued to destroy Hitt-Man's statue with his sledgehammer.

***

It was lights out in the men's correctional facility, so the convicts were either asleep, chopping it up with their celly, or wrapped up in their own thoughts. One particular hardened criminal occupied with mulling over his thoughts was Kyjuan. He was laid back on his bunk, picking the dirt out of his fingernails with a six-inch shank.

Ever since he'd taken the role of OG's top goon, he'd been eating like a fat rat in a cheese factory. He didn't want or need shit. The old head made sure his commissary stayed full, and he had a nice stash put away for a rainy day. Before he'd gotten locked up, he was putting in the same work that he was for OG out in the streets for a local drug baron. The only difference now was, he was using a prison-made knife instead of his gun of choice, which was a .380 ACP. The crazy part about it was, he was making a more substantial amount of money inside than he was during his time on the streets. On top of that, he didn't really fuck with homie he was working for in the hood. It was all business for him. His relationship with OG was different. He really fucked with old dude. He'd shown him love since he'd touched the yard, making sure he had the necessities as well as the extras he wanted. And he didn't want a damn thing in return besides his loyalty.

Kyjuan and OG had grown significantly close since his incarceration. The old man treated him like he was his son, and in turn, he respected him like he was his father. They were fucking with each other like they shared the same bloodline. In fact, they'd even gotten each other's name inked on them to solidify their family bond.

Feeling the vibration of his contraband cellphone in its hiding place, Kyjuan took the time to pull it out and hook up his earphones to it.

"Yo, hold on for a second," Kyjuan told the caller. He got off his bunk to see if OG was asleep. When he glanced at him, his eyes were closed and he was snoring softly. After he confirmed the old man was asleep, he settled back down on his bunk and started back picking his fingernails again. "What up? Nah, I hadda check to make sure my celly was asleep. I'm straight, loved one. I don't need shit. Like I told you before, the old man is keeping me well fed. Yes, sir." He nodded as he thought about the bankrolls of dirty money and commissary he was sitting on. "I'm right under 'em. A nigga done gained his trust, respect, and everything else. Believe me." He nodded and listened to what he was being told.

"I know you said that nigga Hellraiser is on the outside now. And when he finds out that we knocked off his son and his bitch-ass homeboy, he's gonna come seeking revenge," the caller assured him. "I don't give a fuck about that vow he made to God to live a non-violent life. He still has that gangsta shit in 'em, so he's gonna react. That old ass nigga is gonna want blood. Best believe that."

"Facts."

"He and I are definitely gonna dance, and should I just so happen to be the one that loses, I want chu to take out the old man," the caller told him. "You think you can do that for me? Or should I get someone else to handle the job? I know you said you and that old nigga have grown close. I wouldn't want your feelings to get in the way of completing the task."

Kyjuan's heart started beating fast when the idea was brought up of him crushing OG. Though he fucked with the old man, he wasn't of his blood like the caller was.

"Yeah, I can do that," Kyjuan replied, still picking his fingernails.

"Nigga, are you sure? If you can't, I gotta couple of animals on the inside that don't mind getting bloody."

"I'ma handle it. Don't even worry about it."

"Thata boy," the caller said jovially. "Look here, I'ma make it worth yo' while. How does twenty gees sound? I can have that dropped off to yo' BM with no problem. Shit, as a matter of fact, you good for it, bro. I can hit her with that purse tonight."

"Nah, don't wet it. You took care of me since I touched down in here," Kyjuan reminded the caller. "If I'ma do this, then I'ma do it on the love."

"My nigga, love," the caller said happily.

"Love. Peace." Kyjuan disconnected the call, powered off his jack, and stashed it back in its hiding place. He then held up the shank before his eyes and imagined himself putting it through OG's chest. His mind was bombarded with images of the old man wincing and hollering in pain. The thought of inflicting so much pain on a nigga brought him great joy. He was a killa at heart. So, the anticipation of putting in work excited him like new pussy.

***

Zekey pulled up in the driveway of his house and killed the engine of his truck. He, Quan, and Ali hopped out, making their way across the front lawn. He hung his arms around their necks as they proceeded to the front door of their home. They were ignorant to the presence of the van parked directly across the street from

174

them. It had been outside their crib for hours, waiting for someone to come home. Its occupants were five masked gunmen dressed in all black, with night-vision goggles sitting at the top of their heads. They were busy loading their machine guns, when Zekey and his family had arrived. Each man present and accounted for was more dangerous than the next. They were all coldblooded killaz and pledged their loyalty to one man—Changa—Travieso's uncle.

"Okay, they're inside. Let's go," the driver said to the killaz in Spanish. He had just seen Zekey and his family go in the house and shut the door.

All the masked gunmen hopped out the van and crouched down. Together, they hurriedly made their way across the street, looking in both directions.

The Grim Reaper had arrived to claim the lives of Zekey and his family. And the sad part about it was, they didn't even know he was coming.

To Be Concluded
The Last of the OGs 3
Coming Soon...

Submission Guideline

Submit the first three chapters of your completed manuscript to ldpsubmissions@gmail.com, subject line: Your book's title. The manuscript must be in a .doc file and sent as an attachment. Document should be in Times New Roman, double spaced and in size 12 font. Also, provide your synopsis and full contact information. If sending multiple submissions, they must each be in a separate email.

Have a story but no way to send it electronically? You can still submit to LDP/Ca$h Presents. Send in the first three chapters, written or typed, of your completed manuscript to:

LDP: Submissions Dept
Po Box 944
Stockbridge, Ga 30281

DO NOT send original manuscript. Must be a duplicate.

Provide your synopsis and a cover letter containing your full contact information.

Thanks for considering LDP and Ca$h Presents.

The Last of the OGs 2

Coming Soon from Lock Down Publications/Ca$h Presents

BOW DOWN TO MY GANGSTA

By **Ca$h**

TORN BETWEEN TWO

By **Coffee**

THE STREETS STAINED MY SOUL **II**

By **Marcellus Allen**

BLOOD OF A BOSS **VI**

SHADOWS OF THE GAME II

TRAP BASTARD II

By **Askari**

LOYAL TO THE GAME **IV**

By **T.J. & Jelissa**

IF LOVING YOU IS WRONG… **III**

By **Jelissa**

TRUE SAVAGE **VIII**

MIDNIGHT CARTEL IV

DOPE BOY MAGIC IV

CITY OF KINGZ III

By **Chris Green**

BLAST FOR ME **III**

A SAVAGE DOPEBOY III

CUTTHROAT MAFIA III

DUFFLE BAG CARTEL VI

HEARTLESS GOON VI

By **Ghost**

A HUSTLER'S DECEIT III

KILL ZONE **II**

BAE BELONGS TO ME III

Tranay Adams

A DOPE BOY'S QUEEN III
By **Aryanna**
COKE KINGS V
KING OF THE TRAP III
By **T.J. Edwards**
GORILLAZ IN THE BAY V
3X KRAZY III
De'Kari
THE STREETS ARE CALLING II
Duquie Wilson
KINGPIN KILLAZ IV
STREET KINGS III
PAID IN BLOOD III
CARTEL KILLAZ IV
DOPE GODS III
Hood Rich
SINS OF A HUSTLA II
ASAD
KINGZ OF THE GAME VI
Playa Ray
SLAUGHTER GANG IV
RUTHLESS HEART IV
By Willie Slaughter
FUK SHYT II
By Blakk Diamond
TRAP QUEEN
RICH $AVAGE II
By Troublesome
YAYO V
GHOST MOB II

Stilloan Robinson
KINGPIN DREAMS III
By Paper Boi Rari
CREAM III
By Yolanda Moore
SON OF A DOPE FIEND III
HEAVEN GOT A GHETTO II
By Renta
FOREVER GANGSTA II
GLOCKS ON SATIN SHEETS III
By Adrian Dulan
LOYALTY AIN'T PROMISED III
By Keith Williams
THE PRICE YOU PAY FOR LOVE III
By Destiny Skai
I'M NOTHING WITHOUT HIS LOVE II
SINS OF A THUG II
By Monet Dragun
LIFE OF A SAVAGE IV
MURDA SEASON IV
GANGLAND CARTEL IV
CHI'RAQ GANGSTAS IV
KILLERS ON ELM STREET III
JACK BOYZ N DA BRONX II
A DOPEBOY'S DREAM II
By **Romell Tukes**
QUIET MONEY IV
EXTENDED CLIP III
THUG LIFE IV

Tranay Adams

By **Trai'Quan**
THE STREETS MADE ME III
By **Larry D. Wright**
IF YOU CROSS ME ONCE II
ANGEL III
By **Anthony Fields**
FRIEND OR FOE III
By **Mimi**
SAVAGE STORMS III
By **Meesha**
BLOOD ON THE MONEY III
By **J-Blunt**
THE STREETS WILL NEVER CLOSE II
By **K'ajji**
NIGHTMARES OF A HUSTLA III
By **King Dream**
IN THE ARM OF HIS BOSS
By **Jamila**
MONEY, MURDER & MEMORIES III
Malik D. Rice
CONCRETE KILLAZ II
By **Kingpen**
HARD AND RUTHLESS II
By **Von Wiley Hall**
LEVELS TO THIS SHYT II
By **Ah'Million**
MOB TIES II
By **SayNoMore**
BODYMORE MURDERLAND II
By **Delmont Player**

180

THE LAST OF THE OGS III
Tranay Adams
FOR THE LOVE OF A BOSS II
By C. D. Blue

Available Now

RESTRAINING ORDER **I & II**
By **CA$H & Coffee**
LOVE KNOWS NO BOUNDARIES **I II & III**
By **Coffee**
RAISED AS A GOON I, II, III & IV
BRED BY THE SLUMS I, II, III
BLAST FOR ME I & II
ROTTEN TO THE CORE I II III
A BRONX TALE I, II, III
DUFFLE BAG CARTEL I II III IV V
HEARTLESS GOON I II III IV V
A SAVAGE DOPEBOY I II
DRUG LORDS I II III
CUTTHROAT MAFIA I II
By **Ghost**
LAY IT DOWN **I & II**
LAST OF A DYING BREED I II
BLOOD STAINS OF A SHOTTA I & II III
By **Jamaica**
LOYAL TO THE GAME I II III
LIFE OF SIN I, II III

Tranay Adams

By **TJ & Jelissa**
BLOODY COMMAS I & II
SKI MASK CARTEL I II & III
KING OF NEW YORK I II,III IV V
RISE TO POWER I II III
COKE KINGS I II III IV
BORN HEARTLESS I II III IV
KING OF THE TRAP I II

By **T.J. Edwards**
IF LOVING HIM IS WRONG...I & II
LOVE ME EVEN WHEN IT HURTS I II III

By **Jelissa**
WHEN THE STREETS CLAP BACK I & II III
THE HEART OF A SAVAGE I II III

By **Jibril Williams**
A DISTINGUISHED THUG STOLE MY HEART I II & III
LOVE SHOULDN'T HURT I II III IV
RENEGADE BOYS I II III IV
PAID IN KARMA I II III
SAVAGE STORMS I II

By **Meesha**
A GANGSTER'S CODE I &, II III
A GANGSTER'S SYN I II III
THE SAVAGE LIFE I II III
CHAINED TO THE STREETS I II III
BLOOD ON THE MONEY I II

By J-Blunt
PUSH IT TO THE LIMIT

By **Bre' Hayes**
BLOOD OF A BOSS **I, II, III, IV, V**

182

The Last of the OGs 2

SHADOWS OF THE GAME

TRAP BASTARD

By **Askari**

THE STREETS BLEED MURDER **I, II & III**

THE HEART OF A GANGSTA I II& III

By **Jerry Jackson**

CUM FOR ME I II III IV V VI

An **LDP Erotica Collaboration**

BRIDE OF A HUSTLA **I II & II**

THE FETTI GIRLS **I, II& III**

CORRUPTED BY A GANGSTA I, II III, IV

BLINDED BY HIS LOVE

THE PRICE YOU PAY FOR LOVE I II

DOPE GIRL MAGIC I II III

By **Destiny Skai**

WHEN A GOOD GIRL GOES BAD

By **Adrienne**

THE COST OF LOYALTY I II III

By Kweli

A GANGSTER'S REVENGE **I II III & IV**

THE BOSS MAN'S DAUGHTERS I II III IV V

A SAVAGE LOVE **I & II**

BAE BELONGS TO ME I II

A HUSTLER'S DECEIT I, II, III

WHAT BAD BITCHES DO I, II, III

SOUL OF A MONSTER I II III

KILL ZONE

A DOPE BOY'S QUEEN I II

By **Aryanna**

A KINGPIN'S AMBITON

183

Tranay Adams

A KINGPIN'S AMBITION **II**

I MURDER FOR THE DOUGH

By **Ambitious**

TRUE SAVAGE I II III IV V VI VII

DOPE BOY MAGIC I, II, III

MIDNIGHT CARTEL I II III

CITY OF KINGZ I II

By **Chris Green**

A DOPEBOY'S PRAYER

By **Eddie "Wolf" Lee**

THE KING CARTEL **I, II & III**

By **Frank Gresham**

THESE NIGGAS AIN'T LOYAL **I, II & III**

By **Nikki Tee**

GANGSTA SHYT **I II &III**

By **CATO**

THE ULTIMATE BETRAYAL

By **Phoenix**

BOSS'N UP **I , II & III**

By **Royal Nicole**

I LOVE YOU TO DEATH

By Destiny J

I RIDE FOR MY HITTA

I STILL RIDE FOR MY HITTA

By **Misty Holt**

LOVE & CHASIN' PAPER

By **Qay Crockett**

TO DIE IN VAIN

SINS OF A HUSTLA

By **ASAD**

BROOKLYN HUSTLAZ

By **Boogsy Morina**

BROOKLYN ON LOCK I & II

By **Sonovia**

GANGSTA CITY

By **Teddy Duke**

A DRUG KING AND HIS DIAMOND I & II III

A DOPEMAN'S RICHES

HER MAN, MINE'S TOO I, II

CASH MONEY HO'S

THE WIFEY I USED TO BE I II

By Nicole Goosby

TRAPHOUSE KING **I II & III**

KINGPIN KILLAZ I II III

STREET KINGS I II

PAID IN BLOOD **I II**

CARTEL KILLAZ I II III

DOPE GODS I II

By **Hood Rich**

LIPSTICK KILLAH **I, II, III**

CRIME OF PASSION I II & III

FRIEND OR FOE I II

By **Mimi**

STEADY MOBBN' **I, II, III**

THE STREETS STAINED MY SOUL

By **Marcellus Allen**

WHO SHOT YA **I, II, III**

SON OF A DOPE FIEND I II

HEAVEN GOT A GHETTO

Renta

Tranay Adams

GORILLAZ IN THE BAY **I II III IV**

TEARS OF A GANGSTA I II

3X KRAZY I II

DE'KARI

TRIGGADALE I II III

Elijah R. Freeman

GOD BLESS THE TRAPPERS I, II, III

THESE SCANDALOUS STREETS I, II, III

FEAR MY GANGSTA I, II, III IV, V

THESE STREETS DON'T LOVE NOBODY I, II

BURY ME A G I, II, III, IV, V

A GANGSTA'S EMPIRE I, II, III, IV

THE DOPEMAN'S BODYGAURD I II

THE REALEST KILLAZ I II III

THE LAST OF THE OGS I II

Tranay Adams

THE STREETS ARE CALLING

Duquie Wilson

MARRIED TO A BOSS... I II III

By Destiny Skai & Chris Green

KINGZ OF THE GAME I II III IV V

Playa Ray

SLAUGHTER GANG I II III

RUTHLESS HEART I II III

By Willie Slaughter

FUK SHYT

By Blakk Diamond

DON'T F#CK WITH MY HEART I II

By Linnea

ADDICTED TO THE DRAMA I II III

186

The Last of the OGs 2

IN THE ARM OF HIS BOSS II

By Jamila

YAYO I II III IV

A SHOOTER'S AMBITION I II

By S. Allen

TRAP GOD I II III

RICH $AVAGE

By Troublesome

FOREVER GANGSTA

GLOCKS ON SATIN SHEETS I II

By Adrian Dulan

TOE TAGZ I II III

LEVELS TO THIS SHYT

By Ah'Million

KINGPIN DREAMS I II

By Paper Boi Rari

CONFESSIONS OF A GANGSTA I II III

By Nicholas Lock

I'M NOTHING WITHOUT HIS LOVE

SINS OF A THUG

By Monet Dragun

CAUGHT UP IN THE LIFE I II III

By Robert Baptiste

NEW TO THE GAME I II III

MONEY, MURDER & MEMORIES I II

By **Malik D. Rice**

LIFE OF A SAVAGE I II III

A GANGSTA'S QUR'AN I II III

MURDA SEASON I II III

GANGLAND CARTEL I II III

Tranay Adams

CHI'RAQ GANGSTAS I II III
KILLERS ON ELM STREET I II
JACK BOYZ N DA BRONX
A DOPEBOY'S DREAM
By **Romell Tukes**
LOYALTY AIN'T PROMISED I II
By Keith Williams
QUIET MONEY I II III
THUG LIFE I II III
EXTENDED CLIP I II
By **Trai'Quan**
THE STREETS MADE ME I II
By **Larry D. Wright**
THE ULTIMATE SACRIFICE I, II, III, IV, V, VI
KHADIFI
IF YOU CROSS ME ONCE
ANGEL I II
By **Anthony Fields**
THE LIFE OF A HOOD STAR
By Ca$h & Rashia Wilson
THE STREETS WILL NEVER CLOSE
By K'ajji
CREAM I II
By Yolanda Moore
NIGHTMARES OF A HUSTLA I II
By King Dream
CONCRETE KILLAZ
By Kingpen
HARD AND RUTHLESS
By Von Wiley Hall

188

The Last of the OGs 2

GHOST MOB II

Stilloan Robinson

MOB TIES

By SayNoMore

BODYMORE MURDERLAND

By Delmont Player

FOR THE LOVE OF A BOSS

By C. D. Blue

Tranay Adams

BOOKS BY LDP'S CEO, CA$H

The Last of the OGs 2

9 781955 270120